Into the Rabbit Hole

Pangaeas Pandemic

Book 4

Books by Micah T. Dank

Into the Rabbit Hole *series*

Book 1: Beneath the Veil

Book 2: The Sacred Stones

Book 3: The Secret Weapon

Book 4: Pangaeas Pandemic

Coming Soon!

Book 5: The Hidden Archives

Book 6: The Final Type

Into the Rabbit Hole

Pangaeas Pandemic

Book 4

Micah T. Dank

SPEAKING VOLUMES, LLC
NAPLES, FLORIDA
2021

Pangaeas Pandemic

ISBN 978-1-64540-378-4

I'd like to dedicate this book to GianFranco, Rosa, Ava, Giulia and Joseph Fanizza.

I'd also like to dedicate this book to my sister Abby and her fiancé David as well as my mother and my great cousin Mary.

Authors Note

I wrote this book back in 2017-2018. At the time, I had no idea how relevant the topic would be in today's day and age. I hope it gives you pause and thought about how we should be really handling things.

Employ your time in improving yourself by other men's writings so that you shall come easily by what others have labored hard for—Socrates

In a society that has destroyed all adventure, the only adventure left is to destroy that society —Anonymous

Chapter One

Dr. Spear stood and scratched his bald head for a minute. He picked up his cup of coffee, which he had spiked with a little bit of whiskey, and took a giant gulp. He looked out across the dimly lit room at his compadres. His 'family' so to speak. In front of him was the head of the five major families that controlled the world. The Schrodhilt's, which controlled finance through the banking system and sat at the head of the table in the City of London, finance. The Magnor family, which controlled the food and seed supply. The Taros, who controlled the military decisions in the world. The Dotpuns who controlled the media empire. Last but not least, the Rorja family from Spain, which controlled everything else. These were the families that made up the Consulate Fortitute Republics. Conspiracy theorists have labeled them the 'Celebrated Fiat Returns' group, in the sense that according to them, they were making billions, if not trillions of fiat money controlling every aspect of life. It was as the matriarch of the Schrodhilt family had said once, 'If my sons did not want wars, there would be none.' Dr.

Spear laughed as he always wished he had come up with that saying on his own. However, at this pressing moment, there was something very important that they had to get into.

"Gentlemen, please take your seats," Dr. Spear said.

"Why have you collected us here together. We're supposed to be skiing in the Alps right now," Dr. Schrodhilt said.

Dr. Schrodhilt had become very lax as of late, and it didn't sit well with Dr. Spear. However, the only way for the 'system' to work was if all the families got along, so he bit his tongue. It was his families' idea to meet at the Devils Island back in 1910 and start to put together a plan on running the financial system. Dr. Spear felt as if Dr. Schrodhilt had felt that they had contributed enough. However, they hadn't, and they hadn't considered the serious problem they were encountering.

"Gentlemen, the signs of our doctrine have come together. It is time," Dr. Schrodhilt said.

"You mean Nibiru is back?" Dr. Rorja asked.

"NO!" Dr. Schrodhilt slammed his fist on the desk. "I mean, no. I apologize that's not it. But as we know, as above, so below," he said.

"As above, so below," they all repeated.

"There are actually two signs that have come forward recently that show it's time. The first is that the ancient

God of the Jews, Saturn has begun to lose its rings which was prophesized. The second, we have discovered our Sun's binary planet. We have waited so long for the technology to find that. It will fit in nicely with the new spiritual doctrine of Aquarius. Two suns now. My dear Dr. Schrodhilt, we have made a breakthrough," Dr. Spear said. "In a few moments I will show you the status of our progression."

"Couldn't this have been done over the phone?" Dr. Schrodhilt asked.

"Gentlemen," Dr. Spear said as he took another huge gulp of his drink and lit up a cigar and turned his focus to Dr. Schrodhilt, "Everybody is aware here that we sunk the Titanic so that the Astor, Guggenheim, and Strauss families would die on the ship. A price to pay, for ushering in our New World Order. Thanks to your finances Dr. Spear, we were able to pull that off, as we had discussed during the Devil's Island meeting off Carolina in 1910. Without the 'opposers,' we would be able to push our agenda through. However, as we all know, this has become unsustainable. The population has grown exponentially. Little bullshit things such as the 'Georgia Guidestones' have not worked. The population has access to the internet and believes countless things about us. War is not lowering the population, although I'm sure it's making the Taros a lot of money. We are at an impasse, there are simply, too many people to control anymore," he said.

"We've put some suggestions on the table," Dr. Magnor began, "What is this that you are talking about, a breakthrough?" he finished.

Dr. Spear took a deep breath and buzzed out.

"Emile, please bring in patient zero," he said.

A few minutes went by and finally the doors opened, and a young man came in with a pretty young lady, mid-twenties maybe, and walked her in. Everything about her was pristine, except she had some scratches on her face, and she was in a straightjacket. The entire room looked at this display in arousal.

"That's fine Emile, thank you," Dr. Spear said.

"What are you going to do to her?" Emile asked.

"I can assure you that I'm not going to do a thing to her, you're more than welcome to watch. If it's ok with your father," he said.

Emile shot a quick glance over to Dr. Rorja. He nodded. Emile wiped his nose and stared ahead.

"Wonderful. Now, what is your name?" Dr. Spear said.

She didn't reply. Dr. Spear frowned.

"I'm so sorry," he said as he pulled the duct tape off her mouth. "What is your name sweetheart?" He asked.

"KILL ME, KILL ME NOW!" She screamed and hit the floor and started rocking back and forth.

"What is this shit?" Dr. Magnor asked.

"Gentlemen, we have been taking the wrong approach all these years. It's not war, famine, poverty, starvation that keeps the population down. It's the will to live. And we have managed to find a way to remove it from people," he continued.

"How exactly is that?" Dr. Dotpun asked.

"All good things to those who wait," Dr. Spear said. "Now miss, I'm going to take your jacket off," he said, as he unstrapped her. Once out of the jacket, she looked around the room wide eyed. She had a look in her eyes that screamed that she wasn't there anymore. She ran to the window and looked outside, but the light was too bright for her. She looked back at them and then back out the window again that lead to an alleyway in the main building. For all this talk about open borders, they were sealed in by a 15-foot brick wall. Also, they were about three floors up. She thought about running but stopped and turned back to Dr. Spear.

"Please put me out of my misery," she said.

"I will do no such thing," he said.

Frantically she looked around the room and saw a letter opener on his desk. She ran up, grabbed it and plunged it into her neck. Blood shot everywhere, and some got on Dr. Spear's jacket. She staggered back and pulled the letter opener out. She had missed the artery, so she was bleeding out slowly. This didn't seem to be good enough for her. She ran full speed to the window she was looking out of and tried to dive through it. Her body got caught halfway through and the window nearly sliced her head clean off. She twitched for a moment before she slumped over dead. Emile's eyes were as wide as they'd ever been before.

"Emile, please bring in number two. Also, please bring me another jacket," he said as he took his coat off and handed it to him. Emile slumped out of the room in search of number two.

"Now see that gentleman, that is ten days after infection. The problem is that the latency period for the 'impending doom' was too long. We have been working on it, and the next person is at two days," he smiled and laughed at his colleagues.

Nobody said a word as they sat quietly and waited for Emile to come back. After a few more moments, he had his jacket and patient two in the room. This patient was also in a straightjacket.

"What is your name?" Dr. Spear asked.

"Get me out of this jacket and I'll tell you," the second patient said.

Dr. Spear frowned but decided to do as such. He un-did his jacket. Patient two looked around the room, by this point Dr. Spear had hid the letter opener. He saw nothing in the room that he would be able to use to 'take care' of himself. He started to sweat and shake. Finally, after a moment of complete neuromuscular loss, he grabbed the straightjacket and tied it around his neck. He then walked to the corner of the room where there was a sturdy coat rack and tied it off to it. Unfortunately, he was too tall, he was still standing on the floor.

"I've got to get out of my skin," he said eerily as if he had just ingested some bath salts. With everyone look-ing, he let his body hang and folded his legs together. After a few minutes, he stopped twitching and just hung there. The self-discipline in not putting his feet easily on the ground was not lost on this group.

"This is brilliant," Dr. Taros said. "What is it?"

"It's the wave of the future. Once half the population is infected, they will start killing themselves one by one. Once this has caught on, the media will spread the story and panic will ensue. It will be chaos. We project that half the world's population will be dead within a month, we just have to work out a few kinks first before we go live with this. Emile, please clean this shit up," he said.

The men all put their jackets on and laughed to one another about what was about to take place. The truth was, the population was becoming much smarter and challenging the establishment. There were also too many of them to control. If they united, it would mean the end of the 'families.' They couldn't allow this to happen.

"As above, so below," Dr. Spear said.

"As above, so below," they all replied.

Dr. Spear wasn't this excited over a plan since the US government made plans to invade Canada and make it the 51st state after WWI, which was Charles Lindbergh's idea. Truthfully Switzerland, where they were holding these meetings, was becoming a den of debauchery. It wasn't lost on him that public restrooms are lit with blue lights so that junkies can't find their veins. NO, he thought to himself, only the strong survive at this point.

"Do what thou wilt," he said.

"Do what thou wilt," they all repeated.

"I am curious though, what exactly is going on?" Dr. Dotpun asked.

"You know how they recently were able to take out a jellyfish protein to make trees glow in the dark so that they won't need lampposts anymore?" Dr. Spear said.

"Yes?"

"Something to do with that," he said. "Remember, as the great Prince Philip once said, "If I were reincarnated,

I would wish to be returned to Earth as a killer virus to lower human population levels," he finished.

They all left to go skiing, while Emile quietly remained back cleaning up the mess. He knew what he had to do. Was there a chance he would be killed if he got caught? Definitely in the most painful way. But sometimes in life you have to do something for the better good. He began planning his trip to Boston in his head.

All great truths begin as Blasphemies
                              —George Bernard Shaw

Chapter Two

Two months later

"We are gathered here today to witness the wedding of Graham Newsdon and Hannah Dean Husker," the Priest began. I know right? A Priest at MY wedding? I did it out of respect for our families. I couldn't help but laugh to myself. "If anybody knows why these two shouldn't be together, please speak now or forever hold your . . ." he was cut off.

"Kiss her already, Jesus," Jackson said. Everybody laughed.

"Jesus is here, but he is not going to kiss anybody," the Priest said to a roar of laughs. "Hannah, do you?" He asked.

She looked at me, smiled and bit her lip. I know what that means. Universal sign for getting lucky tonight. "I do," she squealed and giggled.

"And do you Graham?" He asked.

I turned around and looked at my small wedding. Scanning the faces one by one. Jean, Rosette, Jackson,

Mom, Brayden, LJ, Dr. Cortese & the Triplets, Conrad from Senna Ore. Even Blur Slanders came up for it. There was a seat left open for NP in the front, I got choked up for a little bit, but then remembered that he was fine, and that I would see him again one day. "I do!" I yelped.

"I now pronounce you man and wife. You may kiss the bride," the Priest said.

I turned to Hannah and flung my arms around her and dipped her back and kissed her. Everybody laughed and hollered and whistled. Some pictures were going off in the background. My wedding made the Quincy paper, plus being a mediocre celebrity brings you attention. I let the paparazzi in. Maybe not a wise move, but who gives a shit. We had decided not to have a pants off dance party for our wedding, just a reception with lots of booze and good people. Tonight, I was going to see her Holy Grail. Well, technically the Holy Grail is astrology also. There is something called 'crater' which means cup in Latin. It borders Leo and Virgo. I'm sorry, I can't fucking help myself but talk about this kind of stuff all the time. It must be getting under your skin at this point. I'll try and do better.

We walked around greeting everybody.

"Hey son," my mom said.

"Hey mom. How much have you had to drink so far?" I asked.

"Did you know that in the ancient Persian times, they used to debate ideas drunk and sober. If the idea sounded good during both times, then they said it was a good idea?" She said, slightly woozy and spilling her wine.

"So glad to know that," I said.

"Congrats, new daughter of mine," mom said as she hugged and kissed Hannah. "Did you know that in the early 1900's getting drunk and riding a pig was considered one of the most extreme sports known to man? Have a great time tonight darling," she said and laughed.

Hannah blushed. "Thanks mom."

Next up, Jean came by with his new girl Larisa who was fresh out of MIT with a computer science degree. Very smart, very beautiful.

"Congrats, mon ami," Jean said.

"We're so happy for you Graham," Larisa said.

"Thanks guys, my mother already completely embarrassed the shit out of us though, so you'll have to try a little bit," I said.

"What's there to embarrass you about? You are both so freaking sexy, I can't stand it," she said.

"Is that so, Bi-Curious George?" I asked.

"Shut up," she laughed. Apparently, she was and that's just fine and right up Jean's alleyway anyway.

Next, we made our way over to Brayden and LJ who were talking to Blur.

"Did you know that Richard Nixon got drunk and ordered a nuclear strike on North Korea before sobering up and cancelling it?" Blur said. Jesus, this guy was always at work.

"Hi Blur, enjoying your time?" I asked.

"Very nice religious ceremony. The Judeo/Christian tradition carries on," he said.

"I wouldn't say it's a Judeo/Christian one," I said.

"That's what our country was founded on," he said.

I turned with Hannah to go, then abruptly turned back around.

"The Christian religion is a parody on the worship of the Sun, in which they put a man called Christ in the place of the Sun, and pay him the adoration originally payed to the Sun," I said

"Who said that?" He asked.

"Thomas Paine," I began "And the day will come when the mystical generation of Jesus, by the supreme being as his father in the womb of a virgin will be classed with the fable of the generation of Minerva in the brain of Jupiter," I finished.

"One of yours?" He asked.

"No, that was Thomas Jefferson to John Adams. What influence in fact have Christian ecclesiastical establishments had on civil society? In many instances they have been upholding the thrones of political tyranny. In no instance have they been sent as the guardians of the liberties of the people," I said.

"What's your point kid?" Blur asked, semi annoyed.

"That was James Madison. Those were three founding fathers of this country. I'm just wondering where you get that this was a Judeo/Christian country founded on those beliefs?" I asked.

Blur sat there stunned for a minute. I guess he had never actually thought about this before. He was just so used to parroting what he believed in, that a counter argument was right in front of his face the whole time. Finally, he spoke up.

"To quote C.S. Lewis kid, I believe in Christianity," he said.

I started to smile. This seemed to have irked him.

"What's so funny?" He asked.

"Not that it's funny, but you didn't finish his quote. He says I believe in Christianity as I believe that the Sun has risen. You don't find that ironic in a way?" I asked.

"I'm going to take off kid. Thanks for the invite. Talk to you soon," he said and turned to walk away before turning back. "Oh, I forgot, here you go," he said as he gave me an envelope. We had only asked for money for our wedding, we did not want to get into gifts and shit.

Plus, we had everything we needed, as well as a state of the art Home Alone trap house thanks to Brayden and LJ. I walked over and put the envelope in our money bag where Rosette was.

"I heard your conversation with Blur, Newsdon," she began, "Don't worry about him. It's the Dunning-Kruger effect. The less you know, the more you think you know," she said as she smiled at me. I smiled back, then walked back over to my wife.

"You know, I'm going to teach you all about the birds and the bees tonight baby," Hannah said, she was getting a little tipsy.

"That's a horrible analogy. Most male birds don't have a dick and bees testicles explode after sex, which kills them," I said laughing.

She looked at me perplexed, then giggled. "I love the way you handled Blur, baby. Handle my sin cave the same way later?" She laughed.

"Excuse me?" I said.

"I want you to press my devil's doorbell," she replied.

"Oh, Jesus Christ, Hannah. What the actual fuck," I said.

She started laughing and then made her way over to Jackson and Rosette with me.

"Congrats buddy, you look so sharp in your little suit over there," Jackson said. I couldn't even say anything back to him because when he gets tipsy, he gets a little handsy and likes to punch arms and slap backs.

"You two are just so perfect," Rosette began, "I'm so happy this finally happened to you. We've been through so much in the last two years, I'm just glad that it's finally over and we can enjoy each other. Speaking of enjoying each other, she looked at me, are you two swingles ready to mingle?" She said as she laughed and snorted.

"Sorry, no babe, but go check out Larisa and Jean, they might be into it," Hannah said.

"Jean, ew, no thank you," Rosette started. She was still trying to get over everything that had happened. "I don't know though, Larisa looks good, she laughed. Here you go guys," she said as she handed us an envelope stacked with cash.

"You guys really didn't have to do this," I started.

"Of course, we did dumbass. I'm still calling you Husker for a while until I get used to it by the way," Rosette said to my wife.

"I wouldn't have it any other way," Hannah said.

The party wrapped up and the friends started making their way back to our house. Jean was pretty wasted at this point and so was Larisa. 100% chance they were going to fuck in my spare room.

We got to the house after about a half an hour walk, and I turned off the alarm, walked upstairs and set the money bag on the dining room table. As predicted, Jean and Larisa went into the spare room. Jackson and Rosette would be in the second bedroom. Our honeymoon was happening tomorrow. We sat down on the couch and turned the TV on. Blur Slanders was on, a repeat though. He was talking about how the Chinese were 90% secular at this point and how they were merging with the Tech giants to create social scores and RFID chip people. I turned the TV on to the music channel. 90's alternative rock. Dave Matthews Band. Yes, I'm into the classics. We started listening to the throwbacks, and then Jackson said something that would change the tone and ruin everything.

"Hey bud, why don't you open your letters and see how you did?" He asked.

"Baby! That's rude, you don't have to do that now," Rosette said.

"No, it's fine, I want them to see our card," Jackson said.

"Alright already, I'll do it," I said.

We went through all the cards together and ended up with $20,000. Jean and Larisa gave us $10,000. When I protested, they told me not to wake them up and smack them in the morning.

"Well, now that's good news, we'll finally be able to have our amazing honeymoon that we've always dreamed of," Hannah said. "Baby, there's one card left here, it was in the pouch, so we didn't see it, why don't you open it up?" She asked.

I got up and grabbed it from her hand. This one had no name on it. Odd. I opened it and a chill ran down my spine.

My life is on the line, I need your help Graham. Call 555-2211 when you get this.

I looked at everyone, and they seemed to have imme- diately sobered up. I showed them the letter.

"You can't call Newsdon, this has to be some kind of sick joke. How did this letter even get in the money bag? Wasn't your mom watching it the whole time?" She asked.

"My mom was watching her drinks empty and refill over and over again," I said.

"I think you should call it," Jackson said.

We sat and deliberated for a few minutes. Finally, we decided that I would make the call.

"Hi, this is Graham News . . ." I said as I was cut off.

"Payphone, Quincy Center Station, fifteen minutes," the voice said.

"Wait what?" I asked.

"Fifteen minutes. Do not call this number again," the voice said and hung up.

I told everybody what they said, and Jackson agreed to come with me. We put our jackets on and ran down the steps and sprinted to the payphone, the one fucking payphone that was still there. By the time we got there, it was ringing. Out of breath, I picked up.

"Take the Red Line to Cambridge, get off and walk two blocks," the voice said and hung up.

I slammed the receiver down. Told Jackson, he swiped me with his card, and we boarded the train. It was going to be about a half an hour trip.

"What do you think is going on?" He asked me.

"Not sure, but I don't like it," I said, still slightly out of breath. These damn cigarettes.

We got to Cambridge, and, just as the voice said, we walked two blocks. When we got to the corner, we stopped right in front of Bionic Edge Pharmaceuticals. We talked for a few minutes, and I pulled a cigarette out and lit it up.

"I wouldn't do that if I were you," a voice said to me. I snapped my head back to turn around and saw a face that I couldn't place, but I've definitely seen before.

"Who are you, what is all of this?" I asked.

"You are literally the only person I could turn to," the man said.

"Ok, but what is going on?" I asked.

The man had an envelope and started to reply when he lost it and dropped it on the floor. A flash drive came out. I bent over to pick it up, then noticed a pattern in his shoelaces. I recognized it as what our undercover agents used to do to transmit messages during the Cold War.

"Someone is following you. Who? We can protect you," I said.

"I'm a dead man walking anyway, it doesn't matter," he sighed. "My name is Emile Rorja, and I'm from the Rorja family. You probably have never heard of us, but we are a very influential global family," he said as he handed me the envelope.

"What is it that you want?" I asked.

He sighed and looked around to make sure nobody was following him. Then he stared at the Pharma building for a good minute and shook his head and laughed.

"Maybe this was a mistake," he said.

"What the hell is going on?" Jackson asked.

I finished my cigarette and turned to light another one. I chain smoke when I'm nervous. As I pulled my hand away from my mouth on my first drag, I heard a scream, and then a body landed literally right next to me, dead. Head cracked open. It knocked my cigarette out of my hand. The man's eyes grew wide as if he were on drugs.

"It's already happening," he said.

"What's already happening?" I asked.

The man turned to run, and Jackson bolted after him, caught him, and we stopped. "What the hell was that back there?" I asked as people started to gather around the body.

"Something very bad is going to happen very soon, and there's nothing anybody can do about it," he said.

"What do you mean?" I asked.

"A lot of people are going to die. I really can't say much, they're probably tracking me now. Everything you need is in that file and envelope," he said.

"What is it?" I asked.

"Our last hope," he said and turned and punched Jackson in the stomach. Jackson let him go and doubled back, he wasn't expecting that. The man took off. The police and ambulances came by shortly thereafter. We decided it was best to get back home. We took a cab back home to Quincy to avoid the Red Line. What was in this envelope?

Keep your eyes on the stars, and your feet on the ground —Teddy Roosevelt

Chapter Three

We finally made it back to the house after a traffic filled adventure from Cambridge. I opened the door and walked up the stairs to our home, careful to disable the trip wire at the front door. You can never be too careful these days.

"Hi baby, how did it go?" Hannah asked.

"You wouldn't believe me if I told you," I replied.

"Oh, I don't think so Newsdon. Check it out," Rosette said as she directed my gaze to the T.V and the reporter on it.

A carbon monoxide leak was detected here at Bionic Edge today, causing the death of four contractors. One made it outside to the roof but slipped and tragically fell to his death. Police are still sorting out the details. More information will come when available. For now, this is Andrea Limitone, Cambridge Massachusetts.

I stared at this T.V. and blinked a few times. "That's not what fucking happened," I said to the group.

"What do you mean, mon ami?" Jean said, looking hungover as fuck. He must have just woken up.

"We were in front of the building when we hear someone scream 'take me now' and jump off the roof. It was a suicide, not an accidental death," I said.

"Are you serious?" Larisa asked.

"Absolutely. I was there. Something horrible is going on here, and we need to get to the bottom of this," Jackson said.

I grabbed the T.V. remote and changed the channel. Blur was on T.V. back in Houston. He was talking about inter-dimensional aliens and how the globalists get their power from them. I turned the T.V. off.

"You know it would be nice to turn the T.V. on to this guy without hearing about how DB Cooper became Tommy Wiseau, or how Taylor Swift is really Zeena Lavey's child," I said.

Jean laughed.

"Ladies, I need your help with something," I began. "We were given an envelope from Emile Rorja. There's a piece of paper in it and a flash drive. I have no idea what's on it, but we need to figure this out," I finished.

"Rorja, like from the elite Rorja bloodline?" Jean asked.

"Since when do you listen to Blur?" I asked him.

"I'm around you enough to pick shit up," he replied.

"Hand it over baby," Hannah said.

"Just one second Hannah!" I said sharply. I immediately regretted it.

"You know that Aaron Burr killed Alexander Hamilton? Well 30 years later Burr's wife got divorced and used Alexander Hamilton, Jr. as her divorce lawyer," she finished.

"What does that have to do with anything?" I asked.

"Because women are crafty. So be nice to me, you turd," she said.

I laughed.

"Let me see the flash drive," Rosette said.

"I hope this isn't as bad as Emile made it seem to me," I said as I sneezed.

"The truth!" Hannah said.

Anytime someone says something and then sneezes, Hannah says 'the truth.' It's an old family hand me down. It's cute sometimes.

"You do know that we say God bless you because of Pope Gregory I. In 590 CE, sneezing was the first sign of the plague, so he ordered that it be said. We've been doing it ever since," Larisa said.

"Do NOT make me get into the Church right now, Larisa," I replied.

I handed it over to Rosette, and she plugged it into her computer. I pulled out the piece of paper. It just had one word on it, well, if you could call it that.

Vizipexmsrw

"Dammit, there's a password on this," Rosette said.

"Let me see that real quick," Larisa replied.

She walked over to Rosette and smiled, brushed her hair back and sat on the couch next to her. She gently took the computer from her and looked at it. She started fumbling around with it.

"What's going on over there?" I asked.

"One sec Graham," she began. "Shit guys, there's a self-destruct on this," she finished.

"What does that mean, ma cherie?" Jean asked.

"It means that if you do not guess the password correctly, it will wipe all the data off it. A bit extreme, I don't usually run into this," she said and frowned.

I looked at the paper again. "Maybe it has something to do with this," I said.

Everybody looked at the sheet of paper with the big bold jumble of letters on the page and tried to figure out what it was.

"This is going to be such a pain in the ass," Rosette started, "There are literally no clues. And we can't enter an incorrect password in the computer, or we'll lose everything," she finished.

We put the password on the whiteboard we had in the living room that we used to decode so many things in the past. If that whiteboard could talk, man the shit it would say.

"Anybody have any ideas?" I asked.

Larisa fumbled around with the computer a little bit more.

"There's no way around this. It's locked tight. I can't reset the computer without losing anything, and there's no work around available on this. If only there was a keystroke indicator on it, I could have accessed it and figured this out. UGH, this is frustrating," Larisa said as she put the computer down for a minute and looked up at the word.

Vizipexmsrw

Larisa stood up slowly and walked towards the board. She then pulled her cell phone out and looked up something.

"Something is oddly familiar about this," she said.

"Jackson, what are you reading or working on these days?" I asked, trying to buy Larisa some time.

"A few things honestly. First, the Big Bang is not the beginning of the universe. Second, Scientists recently created a molecule that can store solar energy for up to 18 years," he said.

"Well why 18?" I asked.

"Well . . ." Jackson began, then was cut off by his girlfriend.

"Because when it turns 18, it goes to the Gentleman's Quarters," Rosette said laughing.

I laughed and pulled up my own computer. I went to Aquastream and checked the latest video of myself. I don't know why I torture myself with looking up videos of what people say about me. It's a horrible habit that can lead to no good, I'm aware of it, but it's strangely addicting. I've been called the literal anti-Christ for the videos I've made. The Westboro Baptist Church demonstrates constantly outside my book signings on my book tour. Sometimes I sit back and can't really grasp what has happened to me, to us in the last two years.

"Newsdon, I've been thinking about that person that jumped off the roof. If you were going to kill yourself, how would you do it? Me personally, it would be having sex for 72 hours straight," Rosette said.

I was about to make a joke to her, but I turned the moment serious like an idiot.

"I've thought about this before. There was a book by an author named Jack London called 'Martin Eden.' It was the story about a man who fell in love with someone out of his wealth class. He tried to get a writing career off the ground and came with rejection after rejection. Including her rejection. Finally, one of his pieces got published, and suddenly the demand for him grew. He was invited to all these fancy places with important people. They even offered him an exorbitant amount of money for his previous work that had been rejected. He realized when he got to that level of success, money, fame and status, that it was all fake. He's on a boat and he decides he can't take it anymore. He slips into the water and then takes a deep breath and dives down as far as he can. But he still has air in his lungs, so his body forces him above the water, and he gasps for breath. By this time, the boat is long gone, and it's just him. He sits for a few minutes, then takes a deep breath, lets it all out, then with no air in his lungs, swims down as far as he can. Once down there, he has no air left to get back up, and he just starts going to sleep, dozing out of consciousness until everything is black," I paused for a moment, "Sometimes that's how I feel when it comes to my writing and speaking career. I wonder if this all isn't just something fake, and I'm going to be found out sooner than later as a fraud," I finished.

Everybody just stopped what they were doing and looked over at me.

"That shit's deep, Newsdon," Rosette began, "But it's nothing new. In psychology it's called the Imposter phenomenon. It's when a person questions their accomplishments and faces anxiety of being exposed as a 'fraud.' It's pretty common with people who achieve success, while others who are equally talented don't," she finished.

"Well that's a relief," I said.

"What have you been working on with your next book?" Jackson asked.

I took a minute. "Well, honestly, about the pole reversal," I said.

"The magnetic pole reversals?" He asked.

"Exactly. See, Walter Russell, the genius that he was broke it down. Everything is Electromagnetism. It's either Electric or Magnetic. Electric is the male energy, Magnetism is the female energy. Electric, radiates, and magnetism attracts. It makes sense if you think about it. See the Moon is the feminine energy. First, it controls the tides of the ocean, so it effects the water currency. We are made up of like 150000% water. The moon has a 28-day cycle, much like women who have 28-day cycles as well. It's not a coincidence. Also, when men orgasm, it feels like a rush of electricity is going through their body, while women who orgasm tend to say it feels more like a wave that they can ride," I finished.

Larisa stopped what she was doing and looked up. "Have you ever had a female orgasm Graham?" She asked.

"I can't say that I have," I replied.

"Well I can tell you from having them, and giving them too, that you're actually right about that," she said.

Jean looked over to her and smiled. He absolutely loves when she talks about other women like that. I haven't seen him this excited over a girl since Dominica.

"I got something guys," Larisa started, "I can't believe I didn't see it before," she said as she sat back down on the couch next to Rosette.

"What is it?" I asked.

"It's written in Caesarian code. I learned about this in undergrad, we had to take a class on secret codes. Basically, what you have to do is move each letter over four letters. It's how they used to communicate under Caesar," she said.

"That's brilliant, why would Emile do that?" Jackson asked.

"Because he probably knew if he got caught, they wouldn't be able to figure it out. This hasn't been used in Millenia," Larisa said.

"Well, what does it say when you translate it," I asked.

"Hold on, I'm doing it," she said. After a minute she put her pen down and looked up to us. "Revelations," she said.

We all went quiet.

"Like the Book of Revelations? The end of the world?" Rosette asked.

"Exactly," Larisa said.

She typed the password in, and the drive opened up. There was a word document and a picture.

"How do you know all of this stuff with computers?" Rosette asked.

"Who was your hero growing up?" Larisa replied.

"Probably the guys from the Rising," she replied and laughed.

"Well, mine was John McAfee and Kim dot com," Larisa replied.

"Who?" Jackson asked.

"They're hackers and anti-virus creators," Larisa said.

"What does the document say?" I asked.

Seek the caged flower, in her mind are passages that will come to pass from her book of secrets. Mention me.

Take the fear out of the age of the people with no written history. Brothers till the end of time. Eye see DDC in the brothers. It's the poison within. Find the cure.

"What in the living fuck does any of that mean?" Rosette asked.

"Not sure, open the picture please," I said.

"You got it," Larisa said.

"Oh, Jesus Christ," I said.

"That's exactly who that is," Rosette said.

"I don't understand how everything in my life has to revolve around this stuff," I exasperated.

"What does it mean?" Jackson said.

"Well first of all, Jesus has the Sun behind him because that's what he represents. He is God's Sun. This is nothing new. He's making the shape of the cross, which is made when you connect December 21, March 21, June 21, September 21. The crown of thorns comes from the Sun's rays, which are not actually on the Sun here but around his heart. Also, the heart is always depicted outside the body of Jesus in pictures because it symbolizes Christ Consciousness. Countless bible verses say that it's found in your heart."

"Well why his picture? Are they saying that he's going to be coming back for Revelations?" Hannah asked.

"Jesus is NOT coming back. Well, technically for another 22,000 years, until we're in Pisces again, if we can even survive ourselves. With all these nuclear weapons on the planet, it can't be good. That's basically how Mars was evaporated. With a nuclear weapon. Also, Revelations is nonsense," I said.

"How's that?" Jackson asked.

"Revelations 12: A great sign appeared in heaven: a woman clothed with the sun, with the moon under her feet and a crown of twelve stars on her head. She was pregnant and cried out in pain as she was about to give birth. Then another sign appeared in heaven: an enormous red dragon with seven heads and ten horns and seven crowns on its heads. Its tail swept a third of the stars out of the sky and flung them to the earth. It's the same thing I've been saying all along. Rosette, what do you think that means?" I asked.

"It basically says, according to this interpretation, Revelation 12: describes the remnant of the seed of the woman as those who keep the commandments of God and have the testimony of Jesus Christ. The offspring of the Woman, the Woman's seed, then refers to the saints," she finished.

"That's nonsense. Ready?" I asked. "First the sign appears in Heaven, so we know it's in the constellations. A woman clothed with the sun, so that's Virgo in the sky with the Sun in Virgo, which makes it 2:00-4:00 pm. The moon was under her feet, so if the Sun is in the Sky, the Moon is below the Earth in the northern hemisphere and is shining in the south. The crown of 12 stars on her head represents the 12 zodiac signs. Another sign appeared in heaven: an enormous red dragon. Its tail swept a third of the stars out of the sky and flung them to earth. So, there's a constellation called Draco, which means Dragon in Latin. It spans from Aries to Sagittarius. But its tail spans from Pisces to Sagittarius. That's four signs or 1/3 of the zodiac. That's why it's able to metaphorically fling 1/3 of the stars out of the sky to Earth," I finished. I should include that in my new book, I thought to myself.

"Whether you choose to believe whatever it is, there are people here who are very invested in this shit. What exactly did Emile say to you?" Rosette asked.

"When the body fell, he said 'It's starting' or some version of that," I said.

"What's starting?" Jean asked.

"Apparently a mass suicide," I said.

"Jesus Christ," Rosette said.

"How can you just make people commit suicide?" Larisa started.

"It can happen, believe me," I said as I thought back to the last time I saw my brother James alive before he took his own life because of that cunt Lilac. Oh shit, wait a second.

"Read that to me again please," I said.

Seek the caged flower, in her mind are passages that will come to pass from her book of secrets. Mention me.

"The caged flower. Lilac, in jail," I said as the thought chilled me to the bone that I would have to sit face to face with the person directly responsible for killing my brother and nearly killing me.

"She's in Leavenworth it says here," Larisa said. Rosette looked at her. You could see she was a little bit hurt that she wasn't the one in charge of looking things up anymore now that we had a computer expert with us.

"Kansas?" I asked.

"Yep," Larisa said. "Also, she happens to be the first President that was ever convicted while still in office. I thought that the President can't be arrested," she finished.

"It was a unique circumstance," I said.

"Larisa, book me a ticket to Leavenworth. I'm heading out tomorrow," I said.

"Who's coming with you?" Hannah said.

"It's best that I go alone for this one," I said.

"Well, what are we supposed to do. What if people start dying all around us while you're gone?" Hannah said.

"I don't think it works like that," I said.

I went into my room to pack an overnight bag while Larisa made the arrangements. I knew things were going to be rough once I saw Lilac. What I didn't know was how she was going to scare the living shit out of me and how this was just the beginning of this Bird Box nightmare.

When the human race learns to read the language of symbolism, a great veil will fall from the eyes of men
—Manly P Hall

Chapter Four

I flew into MCI airport, got my bags and immediately hailed a cab. I wanted to pay in cash, so I couldn't be traced, hence why I didn't take an uber. I sat quietly to myself, lost deep in thought during our 17-mile trip to Leavenworth Maximum Security Prison. I was wondering to myself why it was exactly that the former President had to be locked away in a Maximum Security Prison. I figured she had enough power and clout that she could relax her days like Al Capone did. Then again, maybe they did it for her own protection. Either way, she was going to be completely shocked by my going there. I was struggling with the fact that it was this lady's direct fault as to why my brother died. Jean's situation was a little more understandable, but I don't think I could ever forgive this witch for what she did.

We pulled up at the gate to the prison, and I handed the driver triple the amount and asked him to wait for me. I was going to be a little while, but I didn't want to get stuck here with all these psychopaths, waiting for another cab. I made my way inside, where they fully searched me, made me sign in and leave my phone and keys outside. You can never be too safe at this kind of place.

I sat in the waiting room for half an hour, wondering if she was ever going to come in. Finally, she made her way out of the doorway and looked as surprised to see me as I looked pissed off to see her. She laughed to herself and lit up a cigarette. She waddled over to the table I was at, her legs and hands still chained together as she puffed on her cigarette. It seems that the stresses of prison had gotten her to smoke again. I remember when she made a big anti-smoking ad while in office after her husband died. I guess now all bets were off with her being locked away.

"You've got some serious balls coming here kid," she began.

I looked over to her and shook my head, smirking to myself wondering what the fuck I had just gotten myself into. I pulled a cigarette out of my pocket and lit it.

"Cheers," I said to her as I clanked cigarettes.

"Seriously kid, what the hell are you doing here?" She asked.

"Believe me, I don't want to be here anymore than you want to see the guy that got you sent away. But unfortunately, something has come up and I was sent here to you," I said.

She looked at me and smiled. "Which one sent you here?" She asked.

"What do you mean which one?" I replied.

"Which family," she said.

I paused and looked at her for a long hard second. She knew I was coming. How did she know?

"Emile Rorja," I replied.

She looked surprised, then looked up at the TV and laughed.

"Guard, can you turn that up a little bit," she said.

We both turned around to face the TV.

The hunt continues for the person who killed Emile Rorja, the prodigal son of Dr. Olympus Rorja today. Emile was found face down in an alleyway. The preliminary ME report seems to suggest that he was stabbed in his liver with what appears to have been a spear, however this wasn't the cause of death. She suggests that it was scorpion venom that killed him. More information once we have it. Stay tuned.

My thoughts started racing. A spear to his liver. Spear like Cain, spear like what did Jesus off.

"What the hell is going on here?" I asked.

"You have no idea what kind of shit you have gotten yourself into. You have never seen torture the likes of which these families can inflict on you. It's beyond your wildest imagination. Way worse than any MK programming kid," she said.

"Scorpion venom is about 39 million dollars a gallon. It's literally the most expensive thing in the world. They didn't just want to kill him, they were sending a message. Scorpio is the betrayer in the Bible, are they saying that he betrayed them by coming to me?" I asked.

She sat there staring at her nails. Finally, she took a drag of her cigarette and blew it directly in my face. "You have no idea how fucked you are at this point. You thought the President and the Church were tough to deal with, these people will make you beg for death," she said.

"Speaking of that, that's exactly what I wanted to talk to you about," I began. "A person jumped off the building and killed himself while Emile and I were talking. He looked at me and said 'it's already happening.' Do you know what that means?" I asked.

Former President of the United States Lilac Northinly looked at me with eyes as big as the Moon. "So that's what they've decided," she said and shook her head.

"Decided what?" I asked.

"These are all decided in the Big Heaven Room, Graham," she began as she snubbed out her cigarette and lit up another one. Guess I'm not the only one that chain smokes when nervous. "There is nothing you can do about it now. A lot of people are about to die Graham. This is the Book of Revelations come to life," she said.

"I know all about the Big Heaven Room," I said. "Tell me something I don't know. Something about your book of secrets," I finished.

She took a drag of her cigarette. "Alright then, do you know that all the Presidents can be traced back to the same bloodline?" She asked.

"I know all about the Merovignan bloodline. Tell me something else," I snapped at her.

"Alright then. Do you know that the US has a major nuclear waste that's at the bottom of the ocean and that the casing is starting to erode?" She asked.

"From 1946 to 1993 thirteen countries dumped nuclear waste in the ocean. I know that they've discovered a microbe that eats nuclear waste. I'm not worried. God Dammit Lilac, are you going to stop toying around with me?" I asked.

She took another drag of her cigarette. "Fine. You might as well know this before you're killed anyway," she began. "As you probably have guessed by now, there is an elite group of people who are hell bent on drastically lowering the population of Earth. They think it's too populated and too hard to control. In the book there's a mention of a hypothetical virus or rather an anti-virus that would cause mass panic and suicide. It seems that they have finally found it, but they would only have released it if they didn't get the blessings from the Heavens," she finished.

"Blessing from the Heavens? Also, what do you mean anti-virus?" I asked.

"There are signs in the Heaven's that the elite wait for. They think when things shift, it gives justification. Remember when Pluto got demoted?" She asked.

I nodded.

"It was August 2006. Shortly after that a terrorist plot was foiled in the UK getting all liquids and gels banned from air travel. This was a way to take away even more rights of passengers. They were never going to be allowed to carry out the attack, but they allowed them to plot it to use it to their advantage. Shortly thereafter we did our first flyby of Venus. Things are planned this way. The book mentions a great sign will come to pass that will kick in Agenda 21, or should I say 30 at this point. Then one night, I was watching the TV and they were talking about how Saturn was losing its rings. If you only knew how important Saturn was to them," she said.

"I know all about Saturn, what do you think I do for a living now?" I asked.

"What you don't know is that a virus causes hell on the body, but once infected, the body and doctors fight to get rid of it. It MUST be cured. However, if you fuck around with the anti-virus, then all hell breaks loose. I don't know what they've done, but I can promise you that it's going to look like Armageddon out there in a very short time," she said as she snubbed out her cigarette. The guard started walking towards her slowly. She noticed him out of the corner of her eye.

"Well kid, it looks like it's time for me to go. Good luck with everything," she said as she stood up and turned around to leave.

I sat there for a minute trying to compose my thoughts and realize what she had told me. An anti-virus is going to cause people to kill themselves. How is that even possible? I stood up and walked out of the room and made my way out of the jail. I hopped into my cab and went back to the airport and hopped on a flight back to Boston. How are we going to be able to track this down?

It is hard to free fools from the chains they revere
—Voltaire

Chapter Five

Dr. Spear stood in front of his colleagues eagerly ready to share the good news.

"Gentlemen, it seems that we are ready to put this plan into action," he said.

"It's about time, Dr. Magnor said. "When this goes off, nobody is going to know who to blame. We'll be able to pit country against country. It will be like the Sum of All Fears, except it will actually work. Business will be great," he said.

"That's what we're aiming for," Dr. Spear said. "Now as per our rules, we need to put this to a unanimous vote. Everyone please write yea, or nay on the piece of paper directly in front of you," he said.

He looked across the table at the gold paper and the diamond tipped pens. He smiled. I guess when you have fuck you money, this is the kind of shit you spend it on, he thought to himself. One by one they put the paper in the box. First Schrodhilt, then Magnor, then Taros, then Dotpuns. Lastly, a hesitant Rorja.

"Alright, let's see what we have," Dr. Spear said. One by one he pulled the papers out, four yea and one nay. He frowned.

"Gentlemen, it seems that one of us is not on board with this. I venture a guess who this might be, Dr. Rorja," he said accusingly.

Dr. Rorja scanned across the room. He had to live with the fact that he ordered the death of his eldest son for breaking protocol and for exposing their secret. He wasn't quite sure just how much he had given up, but he was having second doubts.

"Is it really our place to play God?" Dr. Rorja asked.

Dr. Spear turned to him. "My dear Dr. Rorja. I understand completely after your recent loss your feelings on this matter. However, if we do not put this through, his death will be in vain," he said.

"I don't know, Dr. Spear. So many people are going to die because of something we did. How is that justified?" He asked.

"Hell isn't real. The Church has basically declared that. A Pope a long time ago, one that was actually in one of your bloodlines, gentlemen, said 'the myth of Jesus has served us well.' Hell isn't real. Hell is actually on Earth, and more specifically, it's during the Winter on Earth. Once the population has been drastically reduced, we will rebuild. Don't you remember what happened after the Plague? After the Spanish Flu? The population weeded out the weak people, they came back stronger, smarter, faster. Every once in a while, it's necessary to cut the weeds out of the grass, so that the grass may be able to live stronger. The flu was always the answer, we were just too stupid to see it at the time," he said.

"I understand this. But what about Graham Newsdon. My son went to see him," Dr. Rorja said.

"FUCK GRAHAM NEWSDON!" Dr. Spear said as he slammed his hand on the table. "I am so sick of hearing that name. To be honest, it's a miracle he's still alive after everything he's exposed. We won't be making that mistake. I've got great plans for Graham and his friends," Dr. Spear said.

"What exactly do you have planned for him?" Dr. Schrodhilt said.

"Well, we know that he went to visit Lilac in jail. God only knows what she told him. I've put in a call to have her taken out first and foremost. Secondly, we will bring him to the Great White," he finished.

Everyone froze in their seats.

"Did you say the Great White?" Dr. Taros asked.

"I know it's to be saved for the most heinous offenders, but can you honestly name one person alive right now that doesn't deserve it more than this bastard does?" Dr. Spear asked.

Again, silence.

"Then it's done. Let's put this to a vote again," he said as he handed out new paper to everyone. After a minute or two, everybody put the paper in the box, once again Dr. Rorja was last.

"Alright, it's judgment time," Dr. Spear said as he counted them out. Five for five on a vote for yes.

"Excellent! Dr. Rorja, you must never forget. The President, The Royal Family, the Kings and Queens on this Earth, nobody supersedes our divine right to this planet. We have the Annunaki Bloodlines. Remember that," he finished.

"I understand Doctor," he replied.

Little did everyone know that Emile's younger brother, Francis Rorja, was listening the entire time as he had the room bugged once his brother was killed. His hatred for his father was going to have to wait, as he knew it was only going to be a matter of time until they went after Graham. He had to warn them, he just had to be unbelievably careful as to how he was going to do that. His life would be on the line. The Scorpion venom would have killed his brother instantly, but if he was caught, there's no telling what kind of torture he would endure.

Everything we hear is an opinion, not a fact. Everything we see is perspective, not the truth

—Marcus Aurelius

Chapter Six

I got back home around 9:00pm. It was a long and arduous trip back, and I was having trouble staying awake. I opened the door to the house, disabled the trip wire and made my way upstairs. I was stopped immediately once I was upstairs.

"Baby, you have to see this," Hannah said to me.

"What is it?" I asked.

"Just look," she said as she guided my eyes over to the television.

Sad news today coming out of Leavenworth. It seems here that the former President of the United States, Lilac Northinly, has taken her life this evening. Guards found her with a bedsheet wrapped around her neck hanging from the bars. No foul play is suspected here.

I sat stunned. I looked over to Jackson who was busy reading a book, and we made eye contact. He shook his head.

"I can't look at this shit right now," I said and switched the channel to Blur.

What I can't figure out for the life of me is why the mainstream media isn't reporting on this. 38 people dead in Chicago, 74 in Los Angeles and 1035 in Columbia. The last one is being investigated as a ritualistic suicide. We haven't seen anything like this since Jim Jones back in the 70s. All dead from suicide. It's the mark of the beast. What is getting people to kill themselves in large numbers in major cities and countries. What's that? Unfreakinbelievable. I've just gotten word that the death toll in Indianapolis is at 40. To my six million listeners out there, please be careful. There appears to be something out there that is making people take the easy way out. This is terrifying. I'll be here all night bringing you the news on this.

I stood there stunned. It had been two days since my meeting with Emile and seeing that man kill himself outside of Bionic. Now according to Blur, 1147 people have committed suicide. The numbers have gone up exponentially and it's only going to get worse.

The secret of freedom lies in educating people, whereas the secret of tyranny is in keeping them ignorant. That was Robespierre. Someone has to figure out what's going on with these people. Is there anybody out there that is able to help?

I tried to take the focus off the death toll. "Hey Jax, what are you reading there?" I asked.

"Really cool stuff. It's a book called Flicker Men," he said.

"Well what's it about?" I asked.

"Well, you're familiar with the double slit experiment, aren't you?" He asked.

"Vaguely but yes," I replied.

"Basically, this washed up physicist has one last chance for redemption, so he reduplicates the experiment. Things happen and basically at one point he decides to see if everything collapses the wave function. Turns out, no animal can. Humans are the only ones who are able to consciously view the wave pattern and turn it into a fixed point. That's what I'm up to right now, but it's super interesting," he finished.

"Is there ever a time that you're not getting hard for Physics?" I asked.

"Shut up Graham. I don't go on and on when you start talking about the Zodiac, do I?" He asked.

"Did you know that in the middle ages, if you were to be treated herbally, you needed to know your Zodiac sign," I said.

"You're proving my point assloaf," he said.

"Guys, stop arguing please," Hannah said.

"Yeah guys, you're killing the mood in the room. We need to figure out what's going on," Rosette said.

"He started it," Jackson said.

"I'm sorry, I'm just cranky from being awake this long. Also, it seems that every person I talk to ends up dead in some horrible way," I said.

"L'appel du vide," Jean said.

We all stopped talking and turned to him as he was staring out the window.

"What did you say?" Larisa asked.

"There's a phrase for what's going on here. L'appel du vide. In English it's called 'the call of the void.' Have you ever been standing on the train platform, and, when a train pulls in, you had the urge to jump in front? Or have you ever been driving in your car, and you had an urge to swerve into oncoming traffic? Most sane people dismiss these thoughts. Whatever is happening out there right now, people are losing their ability to control that," he said as he pointed to the TV. "Slitting wrists, hanging yourself, jumping in front of cars, drowning yourself. People aren't able to control themselves anymore. We have to figure out what's going on. This isn't going to end well for any of us," he finished.

"You're absolutely right Jean. We have to get focused," Rosette said as she smiled at him. It seems that time has been softening up Rosette to Jean. This was great to see.

The DARPA Avatar project is about transferring consciousness so we can merge with machines and be controlled under the one world government. Everybody will be chipped and controlled like they're doing in China right now.

I turned to the TV. Blur was right back at it.

"Does anybody have a clue as to what we should do right now?" I asked.

Silence.

"Alright, Larisa, go back to the flash drive and see if there's something that we missed. Something, anything," I said.

"You got it, Graham," she said.

"Larisa, I have a question for you," Rosette giggled.

"What's up babe?" She replied.

"When you were dating girls, how could you mess around. I mean, if you each have a 'week off,' that's two weeks a month you can't do anything," Rosette said.

Larisa stopped what she was doing and looked up. "Believe it or not, when you spend a lot of time with another girl, your cycles sync up. It's hormones/pheromones what have you. Spend enough time with me and we'll sync up too," she said as she winked at her.

Rosette giggled.

"Alright, let's refocus before Jean over here has to go relieve himself," I said.

"Tu petite chienne," he said to me.

"Sorry, Jean," I replied.

"Hold on, something just came in," Larisa said.

"What do you have?" Jackson asked.

"It's an email to Graham. Graham, you left yourself logged in to the computer on your protonmail account," Larisa said.

"Well open it, what does it say?" I asked, fully prepping myself for something embarrassing to come up.

"Oh my God. Graham," Larisa said.

"What is it?" I asked.

"You have to read this," she replied and handed it to me over the mini laptop.

From: no recipient

I'm risking my life reaching out to you, but after the death of my brother, I have to do what's right. My name is Francis Rorja. Recently you had a meeting with my brother in Cambridge where he gave you some information. From my calculations you must be at a dead end right now. I can help you. Countless lives are at stake. I can't just sit by and watch as the population turns into Revelations on steroids. I will be in NYC tomorrow. I know your email address is secure, but I can't be too careful. I will be there from 9-10pm, if you do not find me, I'm gone, and you'll never hear from me again. There is a young upcoming Manhattan artist named Gabrielle Roma who is having her portrait gallery tomorrow starting at 7:00 on 27th street. Be there. Hidden in one of her paintings is the location of where you can find me. Everyone wants to park in the shade, but nobody wants to plant a tree. The one who plants trees knowing that he will never sit in the shade, has at least started to understand the meaning of life. I look forward to meeting you. Incidentally, this email contains a virus that will wipe all trace of it on the front and back end within 90 seconds of the email opening. I hope you got all this information. Take care.

Francis

I'm glad I read it out loud, because had I not, I wouldn't be able to repeat it. Not in my condition. I turned the TV back on for everyone. Blur was at it again.

Freaking out over climate change? Do you know how much heat and energy bitcoin mining causes?

I turned away from the TV and told everyone good night. It had been such a long time since I had a good night's rest. Before I went to bed, I spoke to Jackson and he agreed to come with me to the city. We were going to leave Jean back with the women just in case anything happened. What I did not expect was what was going to happen to us next, torture worse than anybody has ever lived through.

If you don't control your mind, someone else will
—John Allston

There's simply no polite way to tell people they've
dedicated their lives to an illusion —Daniel Dennotti

Chapter Seven

We pulled into Penn Station Amtrak top level at 6:00. I was fucking starving, and we had some time to kill. It had been a while since I had good New York pizza. Things I miss about New York, pizza, bagels, bacon, egg and cheese, salt, pepper, ketchup. Until you visit, you just don't know. We went downtown to Grays Papaya for the best hotdogs in the city. Jackson was floored with how good they were, he must have eaten four of them. I looked at my watch, 6:45.

"Alright Jax, let's make our way to the showing," I said.

"I have no idea what we're looking for," he replied.

"Me neither, but let's hope this isn't a trap," I replied.

"I brought the taser brass knuckles just in case," he said.

"Good call bud," I said.

We walked over to West 27th street. I always had a thing for Chelsea in the city. I loved the flatiron building, the sex museum, the pizza stops for a dollar. I loved trips to Eataly and the rooftop bar. The best thing in the city by far is Mulberry Street during the Italian festival. I gain 20 pounds every time I head down there. But I digress. We waited online to get it, it was going to be a packed house tonight.

We made our way inside after about a 20-minute wait online. I checked my watch. Great, we have an hour and 45 minutes to figure this out. They handed out complimentary champagne which Jackson took a glass. I'm still living clean, thank God. We started looking at every single painting, and I noticed a few things. One, this girl is obviously talented beyond belief. Her paintings show women at their strongest, yet most sensitive parts. Drunk in alleyways, on stoops. Passed out in the bathroom. She was just pure Manhattan, this girl. Two, I noticed just how detailed the paintings were. They sprung to life off the canvases. You know how the modern art scene is dogshit? I heard a story about a guy that left a pineapple on a table, and, when he came back the next day, it was encased, and people were looking at it. Another guy took his glasses off and put them on the floor and started staring at them, pretty soon he had a crowd staring at it. And don't get me started on that white on white painting that sold for more than a million dollars. We were staring at a painting of a young woman, sitting down in the shower, naked with her hand over her mouth, when a young woman approached us.

"That's one of my favorite ones," she said.

"It's very raw and emotional," Jackson replied.

"Thanks, I worked really hard on that one," she said as she smiled. "Hi, I'm Gabrielle Roma," she said.

"Wow, so this is your shindig? You painted all of these?" I asked incredulously.

"Um, yup," she smiled and giggled.

I turned to face her and was surprised at how pretty she was. 5-foot-tall, blonde as you couldn't imagine, piercing eyes. This woman was the living embodiment of New York City.

"You're not enjoying the champagne?" She asked.

"I'm good thanks," I replied.

"What does this painting symbolize?" I asked.

She turned and smiled to me. "I never let anybody know my inspiration behind my work," she smiled, as she turned around and walked towards a group of people calling her for some pictures.

I checked my watch, it was 8:15. We didn't have much time left. We started walking around looking at the different paintings. There were women on doorsteps, alleyways, bathroom stalls, all in vulnerable positions, but nothing out of the ordinary. It would take a lifetime to locate those areas. I read somewhere that you could eat at a restaurant every night for something like 20 years in Manhattan, a different restaurant, and you wouldn't have been to them all. There truly is no city like this. We kept walking around, looking until we came up on a TV that was hooked up in the corner with the news on.

"Turn that up," I asked the person closest to it, they nodded.

In what's become the scariest story of the year, a busload of teenagers at Regis Academy have committed suicide tonight. Death toll is up to 25. Police are interviewing parents and teachers to find out what lead to this tragic onslaught of chaos. We'll have more for you as this story breaks.

"We're running out of time," Jackson said, as he looked over at me. Shit, he was right. Before this story, only Blur was covering the news. Now these suicide groups have hit Manhattan. We still had no idea where it was coming about from.

"Come on, we've got to double time it," Jackson said. I looked at my watch again, it was 8:35.

We walked around from painting to painting, growing more solemn in that we were going to lose our only lead. Until we walked up to this one painting that sent a chill down my spine. It was a woman in a miniskirt, laying unconscious on the floor. She was facing the Empire State Building, but she was obscuring a subway stop.

"This HAS to be it Jax," I said. If only I could remember where that spot was.

"Gorgeous isn't it," another girl said to us.

"Huh?" I asked.

"The painting. So, tell me. Do I make a good model?" She asked.

"You're the girl from the painting?" I asked.

"Well, duh," she said and giggled. "My name's Kristie," she said.

"I'm Graham, this is Jackson," I said.

"I know who you are Graham Newsdon. I follow your Aquastream channel online. You lead quite an interesting life," she said.

I hadn't been recognized in public in a different state since that debacle in Arizona. Now, in the city that never sleeps, the only place where famous people can be anonymous, I get recognized. I blushed a little. Then I got struck with a brilliant idea.

"Excuse me Kristie, but where exactly is that subway in the painting?" I asked.

"23rd and Broadway," she said.

"Great, that's just a few blocks from here. We might be able to still make it. Thank you," I said as I turned to walk away.

"Nice meeting you Graham," she said as she smiled.

We ran into Gabrielle Roma at the entrance of the gallery. I walked up to her.

"Thank you," I said as I touched her shoulder.

"For what?" She replied.

"Don't worry about it," I said.

We went outside and started running to the subway, we would make it with five minutes to spare. My lungs were burning though, definitely have to quit smoking at some point.

We made it with three minutes to spare. We looked around at our surroundings. Nothing seemed out of the ordinary. We turned to the subway.

"Maybe he's down there already?" Jackson asked.

Before I had a chance to respond, I felt a poke in my back.

"Keep walking," the voice said. My heart dropped. Did we just get pinched?

Chapter Eight

"Slowly walk down the stairs, don't make any sudden moves," the voice said to us.

We walked downstairs. Once down there we turned around to face this person.

"I'm sorry, I couldn't chance the fact that you had picked up a tail. I knew you guys would figure out where I was," he said.

"Francis?" I asked.

He nodded.

"Ok then, what now?" I asked.

"We're getting on the R Train. Here, use these metrocards," he said and handed us each one.

We got on the train. The car was empty except for a homeless man sleeping at the very end of the cart.

"Why did you drag us here?" I asked.

He took a deep breath. "As you know, my brother was killed. As someone who has also lost a brother to the type of elite power that is going on, I knew that you would understand how I feel. How empty it is. How dry. Your stomach is in knots and you keep wanting to wake up from this horrible nightmare," he said as he looked over at me for some understanding.

I nodded back at him.

"This is only revving up. Tonight, something happened in the city at a very prestigious and very public setting. The spotlight is going to be on this now. Except, nobody is going to know what's going on. It's just going to be highlighted. The panic, the sheer fear and lunacy that will follow, will be unlike anything we've seen before," he said. "Graham, you've exposed so much so far, and for some reason, you're like catching a fish with your hands. You keep getting away. I didn't know who else to turn to," Francis said.

"Why are they doing this?" I asked.

"The official reason, or the off the record answer?" He asked.

"Both!" I replied.

"You're familiar with Nibiru right?" He asked.

"The fictional planet that makes an ellipses revolution around the Sun?" I asked.

"It's not fictional. We had scriptures written thousands of years ago when they first came here saying that they would be back in 3600 years to check on our evolution. Problem is, we haven't. Greed and fear took over. War and death and famine. So, they've decided not to come back. They were supposed to come back this year, and they haven't," he paused for a second. "Basically, the elite families have come up with a new tenement to control," he said.

"What's that exactly?" I asked.

"Off the record, it's population control. There are too many people starving to death, wasting too many resources. You know that the CEO of Nestle said water is not a right for people? That's just the beginning. Basically, this planet is unsustainable the way we are going. Well, I shouldn't say unsustainable. But uncontrollable. People are starting to wake up to this mess that's going on. With the internet, people can research anything they want and follow rabbit holes. Some conspiracies are actually real, the problem is, how to know which ones verses how Blur talks about all of them," he said.

"What's the new doctrine?" I asked.

He took a deep breath. "It's called Kemetism. It's basically a resurgence of the Egyptian religion, but really it's a form of Zoroastrianism. You have been able to figure out a lot of stuff, but there's still a ton that you don't know," he paused. "You know how Abraham was the father of Monotheism supposedly?" He asked.

"Abraham in the Bible was named Abram. Abram is a combination of two words, Abba which means father in Hebrew and Ram, which means Ram in Hebrew. Father of the people of the Ram, Aries," I said.

"Very good, but what you don't know is that Nefertiti in Egypt was practicing monotheism well before the Jews came across it. In fact, Sarah, Abrahams wife is short for Saraswati. Abraham is just Brahma. They are both ripped from Hinduism," he said.

"How do you know all of this?" Jackson asked.

"Growing up in the kind of family that I have, believe me, we had a different education than you did. Now fast forward a little bit. The Jews were originally Moon worshippers. The Moon used to come up behind Sinai at night, and they would see it in the sky. It's why they have a Lunar calendar. Why we have a Moon or Monday. Also, Sinai is a combination of two ancient words. Sin and ai. Sin is the Moon God and ai is mountain. So Mount Sinai is the 'Mountain of the Moon God,'" he said. "At its rawest form, the Jews worship the Moon, and the Christians worship the Sun," he said.

"So, what's going to happen during Aquarius, since the two giant planetary bodies have already been used?" I asked.

"You're very smart, Graham. It's going to get you killed one day, if not by the elite, but by a crazed religious fanatic. To your point, things are too populated right now, and, because of camera phones and the internet, nothing can grow organically. That's why they have to depopulate. To usher in the new Religion for the new sign," he said.

"Holy shit," I said.

"Exactly," he replied.

"I read about a third century Church they uncovered in Megitto, Israel. It's one if not the oldest Church on record. In the middle of the floor is a giant mosaic of the sign of Pisces. Gaianus the Roman paid for it to be there," I said.

"Times were easier back then to control people. However, these days, everybody's got an opinion. Now that we're a global entity, how do you think people are going to get a new way of thinking through," he said.

"But why the Zodiac and the constellations. Why does that HAVE to be the thing that controls us?" I asked.

"Every culture borrows from a previous culture and incorporates things. The same way that DNA breaks in half and then attaches to another to create new life, it's a similar process with religion. Fuck, the word God is literally Dog spelled backwards. Do you know why?" He asked.

I shook my head no.

"It goes back to ancient Egypt. To Anubis, the Dog. It's why Religion has DOGma," he said. "Josephus, who ironically is the one that Christians site for the proof about Christ, he said in his work that the Jewish temple at Jerusalem had the twelve signs of the Zodiac on the floor. Deuteronomy 4:19. Are you familiar with it?" he asked.

"And when you look up to the sky and see the Sun, the Moon and the Stars, all the heavenly array – do not be enticed into bowing down to them and worshipping things the Lord your God has apportioned to all the nations under Heaven," I said.

"You know your shit choirboy. This is where it gets twisted. The constellations and the Zodiac, the signs, the stars, the myths, the stories that came out of them was supposed to be appreciated. In Job, God asks Job where he was when he created the Mazzaroth. You have to realize that our constellations and Zodiac is created especially for us. It's like God's signature. In other worlds, they have different alignments of stars and their own Mythology, but this is ours. And some very powerful people have disregarded Deuteronomy 4:19 and have instead weaponized it," he finished.

"This is too much to process," Jackson said.

"It is crazy to think about it, but Graham you know much of this stuff already. Why do you think there's always a stock crash in Libra?" He asked.

I opened my mouth, but nothing came out. I had never thought of it that way. "Libra is the judge. The Sun comes across the equinox on its way down to its death," I said.

"Exactly, it's the Elite's judging the people," he said.

I held my hand up and paused him for a second. This was a lot to take in. Rosette would say that it's the 'curse of knowledge' principle.

"The Catholic Catechism that you wrote about in your first book that says not to give in to Astrology. That was added to keep people away. But you know better. This is straight out of Saul Alinsky's book "Rules for Radicals." Do something, and then accuse others of doing what you're doing and try and put a stop to it. It's pure fucking gaslighting to be honest," he said.

"I don't know, this is still a little crazy to me," Jackson said.

Francis rolled his eyes. "Jackson, the Jews put the lambs' blood over their door so that the firstborn son wouldn't die. The lamb is the Ram, Aries. The Jews identified their doors letting God know they were Jews. The death of the son/sun. Have you ever heard of Peter Pan?" He asked Jackson.

"Of course," he replied.

"Do you know where that comes from. Or even who he was?" He asked.

"Peter Pan is not real," Jackson said.

"Symbolically," Francis replied.

He shook his head no.

"Peter was the right hand of Jesus. He's the rock that he built his Church on. Pan is a Greek God. One half

Goat, the bottom half, the top half man. That's the two signs, Capricorn and Aquarius. Put them together and he's the 'new age' of Aquarius and Capricorn, the next 4000 years that the new faith is to be built on. Do you know what Neverland is or why the children never age?" He asked.

Again, Jackson shook his head.

"Peter Pan is the Angel of Death. He takes the children to Heaven, where they never have to grow up, and play all day. This was a prophecy. What about Mermaids and Mermen. Do you know what they are?" He asked.

"This one of course I know," Jackson said.

"Did you ALSO know that they date back to Mithra and Dagon, the ancient Gods. They are a combination of Pisces and Aquarius, the fish and the man, the two neighboring signs. The Mermaids however are a combination of the fish and the woman Virgo. The 'opposing' signs," he finished.

"Is everything connected back to this?" He asked. I could see things were finally starting to connect in his brain. I thought back to us in the spiked room in Israel and the password being Dagon. I didn't realize the rest though. I still had so much to learn.

"You asked before what triggered this. Two things. One, Saturn is losing its rings. The first God of the Jews, the first people of the book, the Chosen ones. This symbolizes the end of a time. Also, our Sun's binary Sun had been discovered. Like we are in a binary with Sirius, this Sun now has a binary Sun. The two Suns, or Sons. The twins. Gemini. The people with no history. At least no recorded history. The new religion will be based off Aquarius, but will reflect Gemini as well," He paused for a moment. "You HAVE to understand that the majority of the people in secret societies are Satanists," he said.

"Satan is not real," I replied.

"I watched your Orpheum presentation on that. It was very interesting. A little misguided perhaps, but interesting. Certainly make a good case for it. When I say Satanist, you picture Devil worshipping, human sacrifices, blood and semen drinking, upside down crosses et cetera, et cetera, et cetera. This is NOT what real Satanism is. Remember what Al Pacino said in 'The Devil's Advocate.' He called himself a humanist. That's what Satanism truly is. It's basically 'Do what thou wilt' but with an added 'Don't be a dick.' There are so many misconceptions of Satanism. It was created initially to pound out the flaws in the Church. Also, Satan doesn't harm the innocents in the Bible if you read it correctly, only God does that. They also don't believe in the afterlife so they are against murder, because you would be taking away the only life one has," he said.

"I know the afterlife exists. I've seen it with my own eyes," I said.

"Your DMT trip?" He asked.

I forgot I wrote about it.

"Exactly," I said.

"John Lennon said that the government created LSD to trap us, instead it set us free. If you believe what you saw was real, that's great. My point was basically that all the Freemasons and the lower level secret societies, they're all Luciferians. The Church has corrupted what Luciferianism truly is," he finished.

"What do you mean?" I asked.

"Think about it. I mean there are some who truly believe in Satan, which you have pointed out in your Orpheum lecture which I saw, good job by the way, but you were wrong about one thing," he said.

"What's that?" I asked quizzically.

"Lucifer is not Satan," he said.

I sat for a moment to myself to reflect.

"Lucifer is the Morningstar. It's Venus. It announces the arrival of God's Sun. It's the light bringer. This is the thing that Christians don't seem to understand. Do you really think that the Masons and all these secret societies worship the Devil? Do you really think that it's THAT out in the open?" He asked.

I shook my head at him. I have no fucking clue.

"Revelations 22:16. I am the root, and the offspring of David, and the bright Morning Star. Lucifer calls himself the Morning Star. Why would Jesus call himself Lucifer?" He asked.

Again, I shook my head.

"Light. Jesus says 'I am the light.' It applies for the Sun and for Venus. Jesus is light. Lucifer is light. This is what Christians conflate. They think they have it all figured out, that they worship Satan. Lucifer and Satan became intertwined by the early Church. WRONG. They worship light. Everything positive is reflected in light, everything negative in darkness. It's the duality. Without one, there can't be the other," he continues, "Does the Church also talk about the Bishop who was named Lucifer and was made a Saint? St. Lucifer of Cagliaria fought AGAINST the sweeping Romans but lost. This eventually ended up becoming the Roman Catholic Church. Rome, never fell, it just rebranded itself.

Even though it was making a little bit of sense, it was bothering my stomach. I had been able since my awakening to view my own cognitive dissonance and confront it directly. Maybe I wasn't ready to hop on board with this.

"Go back home and take a look at that flash drive again. You guys are missing something," he said.

Next stop, Times Square. Please remember to take all your belongings when you exit the subway.

"This is where I get off. I've said as much as I could. I wish you guys the best of luck," Francis said as he exited the train and disappeared into the crowd at Times Square, I'm assuming.

I sat there quietly for a moment processing all the information that he had given me, taught me. Things I knew about but didn't realize how much I didn't know about. A thought occurred to me though. That if this is just encoded Astrology and Astronomy, then it isn't divine. If it isn't divine, then that means it was written by a human. The human may have thought they were inspired by God, but this book is clearly more than it appears to be. Also, if this was written by a human and wasn't divine, than the passages about Homosexuality being evil was just a thought of a person that wrote something down. It's not divine ordinance. If only the LGBT community could understand everything that I've learned and maybe agree with me, they wouldn't have to worry so much about their impending fiery trip to hell.

Jackson looked over to me. "I didn't realize just how much is being controlled by all of this," he said. "Alright, I'm in. What do we have to do?" He asked.

"Let's go home and look at that flash drive again. Call up to Larisa and get her working. We have to take this back down one stop to Herald Square and then walk a few blocks to Penn," I said.

We stood up to get off when suddenly two men entered the subway and sat down across from us.

"We've been looking for you," one of the men said.

Chapter Nine

"Who the hell are you?" I asked, a nervous ball in the pit of my stomach.

"Doesn't really matter, now does it," the first man said to me as he pulled his jacket back and showed his 9mm.

"Guess not," Jackson said. "What now?" He asked.

"We're getting off. Don't try anything smart," the second man said.

We got off the subway and walked upstairs. One of the men hailed a cab and we all got in.

"Central Park please," the first man said.

"Central Park and what?" The cab driver asked.

"Anywhere," the second man said as he turned and cocked a half smile at us.

We got to Central Park, and the men led us into the forest by gun. Typical New Yorkers though. Homeless people everywhere, and nobody bats an eye for us or the man with the gun. They lead us to an isolated path, when suddenly we stopped.

"Wallets and cell phones please," the first man said to us.

Reluctantly we took our wallets and cell phones out, but not before I pinged Hannah. After everything we've been through, when I do that it means for her to Ping me back and check on my location. I handed over the phone. The man took our batteries and SIM cards out of the phones and put them in his pocket. He then put his phones in the backpack he had been wearing.

"Now that that's been taken care of, I have just one question for you. Where is Francis?" The first man asked.

Jackson and I looked at each other and then back at them with our hands raised in the air.

"Hello, anybody?" The first man asked again.

"We don't know anything," Jackson said.

"Bullshit you don't know anything. If anything, you know too much," the first man said as he chambered the round and aimed it at my head.

"We don't know where he went. He just got off the subway after he was done talking," I said.

"Where did he get off?" The second man asked.

"Right before you got on," I said.

The men looked at each other, then the second man turned to make a phone call. The first man with the gun just stared at us, I don't even think he blinked. Finally, the second man got off the phone and nodded to the first. The first man released his gun and holstered it back up.

"Keep your hands up," the first man said as the second man walked over to us and patted us down. First me, then Jackson. When he patted his front pocket, he sounded surprised.

"Well, what do we have here boss?" The second man said as he pulled out the brass knuckles with the taser on it. He tested it out, and the middle knuckle sparked up. "Cool," he said. "Alright boys, you're going on a little ride with us," he said as he motioned to the path. We saw headlights slowly start to roll up to us. We walked into the unmarked car, and the man with the gun sat in the front, and the three of us sat in the back, the second man between Jackson and me. They put hoods over our heads so we couldn't see anything.

"That's not going to be good enough, they'll just map it out in their head," the first man said.

The second man said ok. Then I heard a noise and a thump. Suddenly I felt a jolt of electricity roaring through my body like I'd never felt before, then everything went black.

Day 1

I was awoken to the bag being pulled off my head. I looked around. My chest was on fire. Jackson still had his bag over his head. We were tied to chairs in the middle of what I can only describe to you as a completely white room. Like looney bin white room. Every fucking thing in here was white. The men were dressed in all white, the doors were white, the walls, ceilings everything you could think of was white. The second man took Jacksons hood off. I scanned the room until I turned to my right and let out a yelp. That woke Jackson up and he looked over and screamed.

There in the corner of the room on a white tarp was Francis. He was dead, laying face down. His back had been completely sliced open, the ribs broken outwards and his lungs pulled out. I recognized this medieval torture before. This was called the 'Blood Eagle.' His back looked like it had wings. It was done to him while he was alive, and his lungs were pulled out, which slowly suffocated him to death. This would be the same death that people who were crucified would die, slow suffocation. Forget cryptic messages about Scorpion Venom, this went directly to the point. His blood was the only thing I could see that had any color in this room, which is a form of sensory deprivation that has been used on people before. The two men flipped him over and put him on a gurney. They then slowly wheeled him past us and on the way out of the door. As Francis was passing us, his arms came up and crossed over his chest.

"Jesus, he's still alive," Jackson said.

"No, he's dead. That's just the Lazarus reflex," I said. I remember learning about that in medical school for the short time I was there. It scares the shit out of people, it's rare, but it does happen. Named after Lazarus, who Jesus rose from the dead, which goes back to El Azur who was Osiris in ancient Egyptian mythology. All the same shit.

The men wheeled him out, careful not to drop any blood. After all, any color would defeat the purpose of this torture. We waited there in silence for them to come back, both of us too nervous to say anything. If they were willing to do THAT to one of their own, who knows what's going to end up happening to us. After a few minutes, the first man with the gun came back in the room alone. He walked slowly up to us, again, completely in white, even his shoes.

"Gentlemen," he began, "Let me cut to the chase. Your purpose here is to experience maximum torture. Torture so bad that you'll be begging for us to kill you, and we will, don't you worry, but not a moment too soon," he said, gun pointed to us as he took a knife out of his pocket and cut the zip ties to our feet and hands. I rubbed my wrists, it felt good to get out of those restraints. "Now we will see you, but you won't be able to see us. See that mirror over there?" He asked as he pointed to the wall. We nodded. "That's where we are. So, don't try any shit. Any requests?" He asked.

"Can we get something to eat and drink?" Jackson asked.

The man chuckled to himself, then pistol whipped Jackson across the face, his eye started to swell up a bit. "I don't see why not," he said as he nodded to the mirror. "First, put these on," he said to us as he handed us a white jumpsuit and white crocs. "NOW!" He said.

Jackson and I got undressed and put our new clothes on. It was like a Heaven's Gate prison suit.

"You both look great. Ah look, your food is here," he said as he walked out the door and shut it behind him. We heard the door lock.

We looked at the white table that was in front of us. A water bottle with the label ripped off and a quart of milk. Two Styrofoam cups. For food, we had a block of white rice each on a paper plate with plastic utensils, no knife though. They really were taking this white out thing seriously.

"I have to ask you a question, Graham," Jackson said.

"What's up?" I asked as I took a giant gulp of water.

"Remember when I saved you from those men at the Boston Pier, and you asked to be tased?" He asked.

I nodded.

"Well, you've finally been tased. Was it everything you dreamed it would be and more?" He laughed.

I chuckled. We were going to need this sense of humor if we were going to survive this. As I thought that, a feeling filled up in my stomach like I was going to have to shit. I ran to the corner of the room and sat on the toilet and took the biggest adrenaline shit of my life. I flushed the toilet then made my way back to Jackson.

"What do you think they're going to have for us?" Jackson asked.

"I don't know, but I'm going to try and rest for a little bit," I said as I went to the corner of the room and laid on the cot.

"Me too brother," he said, and he went to his. Within a few minutes we were both unconscious.

Day 2

We woke up to a breakfast of egg whites and water. If these people don't stop, I'm going to start leaving Yelp reviews for this hotel. Also, there was a song playing through the ceiling, that I couldn't recognize at first, until I finally did.

"What is that song?" Jackson asked.

"It's the most evil song ever recorded. It was banned in a few countries because too many people committed suicide after hearing it. It's called 'Gloomy Sunday.' This is just a warmup for us. It's probably just a metaphor for what's to come. Or to tease us into asking them to kill us," I said. I wasn't superstitious, but this song was going to get annoying.

5 hours later

This song is still playing. Each hour, they turn the volume up another couple of notches. It's now all I hear, all I think about. I'm slowly starting to lose my mind, then suddenly, it stopped. There was peace and quiet for a few minutes, before I heard the most terrifying screaming coming from the speakers. I turned to Jackson.

"What the hell is that?" I asked.

"I think I know," he said.

"What?" I asked.

"It's something called an Aztec Death Whistle. They're rare, but when you blow into it, it emits a scream. They must have recorded it. I don't know how much more I can take of this Graham," Jackson said.

We sat there for a while and endured the screaming.

3 hours later

"What is that now?" I asked.

"They've combined the two. Graham, I'm going to tear my ears off," Jackson said as he started to rock back and forth. Not a good sign. Also, it takes something like ten lbs of pressure to rip an ear off, and this superman would have no problem doing so. I wanted to tell him that even if he ripped them off, his ear canal is still there, so it wouldn't do much good, but I figured I'd save my energy. I'm just hoping this guy doesn't go semiautomatic on me and rips MY head off. It has become clear to us now that they weren't going to stop with the terrifying noises, and also they didn't feed us for dinner, so I made my way back to my cot and rocked myself as well. I looked over to Jackson and he was sweating, eyes closed on the cot. I wasn't sure if he was sleeping or not, but I was not about to go over there and potentially wake him up. I dozed off after an hour of trying to ground myself.

Day 3

We woke up in the morning and both of us were taped down to a gurney with headphones over our ears. You can't imagine the nightmares I had, and I can only imagine Jackson had. The music had stopped playing at some point throughout the night. The body cools down when you fall asleep, and as you enter deep Alpha and Theta waves of sleep, your breathing depresses. Some point throughout the night when we fell asleep, they must have turned the music on. I remember it being loud in my dream, but then it stopped at one point. They must have a very intricate meter that measures the temperature in the room and know when to turn the music off. The dreams that I had could put the Momo challenge to shame.

"Ah, you're both awake," the first man said. "Good. This is very exciting for me, I've never seen this actually be tried on a human being before," he said as he turned the noise on our headphones. No music though, just light static. It wasn't loud, but it was prominent. I suddenly had a dread for what was about to happen next. "Oops, I forgot something, silly me," he said and walked out of the room.

"Jax, you still with me?" I asked.

"Kind of. What are they going to do to us?" He asked.

"If he comes back with Ping Pong balls, I need you to keep calm," I said.

"Why Ping Pong Balls?" He asked.

"It's called a Ganzfeld hallucination. My brother told me about it when he graduated. They play static in your ears, and tape half of the ping pong ball to your eyes so you can only see diffused white light from this all white room," I said. Now I know why everything has to be white here.

"Alright, I'm back. Hope you didn't miss me. Let's get started," the man said.

The man came to us one by one and taped ping pong balls to our eyes. Then he turned the static on to the point where we wouldn't be able to talk to each other.

6 hours later

We are still on the table, but I feel like I'm floating into outer space. My thoughts are not my own anymore. This is more intense, more real than a DMT trip I took not long ago when I saw NP. Just when I thought I couldn't take it anymore, the man comes back in the room and takes our headphones off. Even though they were off, I could still hear the static. I think the noise is permanently etched into my brain. Next, he took the re- straints off, and I sat up and went to take the ping pong balls off my eyes.

"I wouldn't do that if I were you," the man said to me.

I didn't listen. Static in my ears, I ripped them off and was met with a glaring piercing white light from the light bulbs above. Also, everything was swirling. I fell off the gurney and landed on the floor and grabbed a bucket that the man had brought in for us and started projectile vom- iting in it. Well, not really. We hadn't eaten in a day and a half, so it was pretty much pure bile. I heard Jackson throwing up as well. Once I was done, I pushed the bucket aside, room still swirling, and crawled to the cot where I laid down and tried to pass out. The man left the room. As I was drifting into a very nauseating scream, the sound of the Aztec Death Whistle started blaring through the speakers. I don't know how much longer I can survive this.

Day 4

"Hey bro, you up?" Jackson said.

I opened my eyes. Things weren't spinning anymore, but I was starting to shake. My body was run down, I hadn't micro dosed in nearly a week, so my anxiety was at its highest level.

"Yeah what's up. What time is it?" I asked.

"I've been timing these people coming in and out, and you know what I've noticed?" He whispered to me.

I looked at him and shook my head.

"There's a gap from 3-3:30 where there's no noise, no music, nobody here. They must be switching shifts at that time," he said.

I laughed to myself. 3:00 a.m. is the Devils hour. It's the inverse of 3:00pm which is daytime. They say that only the weird shit happens at 3:00 a.m. It would make complete sense that they switch over around then. I mean, that man can't possibly be here around the clock. When was this torture going to end?

"Stand up," the man said. We hadn't even heard him come in. I think my hearing is all sorts of fucked up now from all of this.

We stood up and the man looked at me and smiled. "I must admit, you guys are much tougher than the last ones that were here. Nobody makes it to day four. But since we're here," he began as he cracked his knuckles and his back, "I have something for you, and I know you're going to be especially happy to see it Graham Newsdon," he said as he put a white paper bag on the table. "I know you're going to like this one," he said and pointed to me to go to the bag.

I walked over to the bag and looked inside. "No, you can't," I pleaded.

The man drew his gun out and aimed it at us. This is where he fucked up. We hadn't been in the white room long enough. His black gun posted a complete contrast to the white everything. Jackson and I were staring at it, as it broke the trance of lack of colors. It was like a breath of fresh life came into both Jackson and me, but I tried not to show it to him.

"Alright," I said as I pulled out the bottle in there. In the bag was a bottle of Snake Venom Beer. It's the strongest beer in the world, nearly 68% alcohol by volume. It's stronger than whiskey.

"I'm going to sit here while you finish it off, Graham," he said.

I shook my head no. He walked up to me, chambered a bullet and put it at my head. I started to tremble from the weight of the torture I had been going through for nearly the past week.

"Alright," I said.

I cracked the bottle and took a gulp. The first gulp I took brought back a rush of memories. Suddenly I was remembering all the College parties at Georgetown that Jean and I were at. I remember even further back to when I had my first drink at 14 in High School in the back seat of NP's car. I remembered all the times I went out with Hannah to restaurants, and she would order a cocktail and I'd have like five beers for dinner. I remembered it all. I pulled my lips from the bottle and got goosebumps. Shit's fucking strong. Jackson looked at me, and I watched his eyes hit the floor and him shake his head. I turned to the man with the gun who motioned with the gun for me to keep going. So, I did.

1 hour later

The man is gone, and I've never been so wasted in my life. Nothing I say or do is going to stick as a memory for me. It's been two days without food, and Jackson is in the corner, possibly crying to himself. Of course, he will not let me see that. Aw fuck, I was doing so good without the sauce. Now all these old feelings come back, and, as shitty as I feel right now, I remember why I missed it so much. When I was hammered, I was free. I had no inhibitions. Problem was, I would always make stupid decisions. Lucky for me, I'm in an all white room with no way to hurt myself. I started pacing around the room, holding onto the wall, on account that I was fucking obliterated. I don't know how much more I can handle.

4 hours later

I'm starting to come down a little bit, but I'm still pretty dizzy. I sat down on the cot, and slowly lowered myself to a laying down position. Still extremely dizzy, I laid down and closed my eyes. Nope, not going to happen. I sat back up and opened my eyes. All I want to do is pass out and not wake up. Just float away. Go wherever NP is. I've seen more than most people on this Earth at this point. Why is it always up to me to save the world?

"Get up maggot," the man was back and yelling at me. He put a white thermos on the table. "Drink this," he said.

"I can't drink anymore, please. I haven't eaten in 2 days and I'm still so fucked up," I said.

"I know, this will help you," he said.

I walked over to him because, what choice did I have. Well, waddle would be a better word actually. When I got to him, I picked up the thermos and took a sip. It was pungent.

"Why are you giving me coffee?" I asked.

"Just drink it," he said.

"Or what? You'll pull your gun out again?" I said.

Right on cue, he pulled his gun out. Once again, it broke me from the pattern of all white in the room. I smiled at him and pounded the coffee.

"What exactly was the purpose of that?" I asked.

"You'll see," he said as he left the room.

I went back to my corner and lay down. Suddenly a rush of energy came through my veins like I've never felt before. I stood up, feeling nearly sober, and walked around the room. At the edge of the room I came across something interesting. They were wall tiles in white, but there were different things carved into each individual one. They all seem to be ancient Egyptian. Go figure. I looked above my head to see this message engraved into the wall.

First the limo saga, then the spa breaker. A blind ordain. No iris. The loan con. The anti-age sane ref. Hail pimp, with tonic, dim ice while in tees.

My brain just wasn't in a position to handle this at this point. I walked back over to the cot and sat down. Honestly, I've never felt so energetic in my life. Then I realized what happened. He gave me a liter of Death Wish Coffee. This stuff is 200% more caffeine than regular coffee. Coffee was discovered in the 9th century by a goat herder named Kaldi. He caught his animals eating the beans and getting anxious. I'm so drunk and tired and all I want to do is fall asleep, but I'll never sleep tonight, not a chance. Just then, right on cue, the Aztec Death Whistle came back on. I sat on the cot and closed my eyes and rocked back and forth. This was going to be a long night.

Day 5

I waited as long as I could handle it before I woke Jackson up. He looked over to me and saw that I hadn't slept.

"I'm so sorry about yesterday Graham. Did you get any sleep?" He asked.

"Not a wink," I said.

"Shit," he said.

"I did find something interesting though, come over here and take a look," I said as I walked him over to the wall. I pointed out all the Hieroglyphics on the wall.

"Now that is interesting. Do you think it will tell us something?" He asked.

"I've been staring at it all night. They don't make any sense. They're not in any particular order," I said.

"You can read Hieroglyphics?" He asked.

"Used to be a hobby of mine, just basic shit," I said.

"Alright everybody, time for your medicine," the man said. He has this habit of sneaking up on us. I felt so weak at this point, something didn't sit right with me.

"What now?" I asked.

The man didn't say anything to me. He just walked up to me quietly, took out the brass knuckles, buried it in my chest and turned the taser on. Suddenly everything went dark.

Chapter Ten

I felt myself conscious in the blackness. All of a sudden, I felt that familiar white vortex pulling me up. After what felt like an eternity, I found myself without a body, but with all five senses completely sharpened, more than when I was fully conscious. I heard an entity begin to speak in my mind.

"How are you feeling, Graham?" The entity asked.

Before I could answer, I thought my answer. I felt the entity read my thoughts.

"I see. You've been through quite an ordeal the past few days, haven't you?" It asked.

"Who are you?" I asked.

"We'll get to that," he replied.

"Where am I?" I asked. I could feel my spirit start to 'get its legs' so to speak, and I floated around.

"You feel that line yet? You should feel a slight pressure," it said.

"I do," I replied.

"Don't fight through it and continue to move. We won't be able to send you back," it said.

"Send me back where?" I asked.

"You're in the 5th dimension again. If you fight through and make the 'jump,' you won't be able to head back to Earth," it said.

"Where am I?" I asked.

"Technically you're dead right now," it said.

"What?!" I asked feeling panic rise, but just as quickly as it started to rise it was completely suppressed. I was free.

"You haven't eaten in three days, haven't slept, been tortured, been beyond drunk and were just tased. Your heart just stopped. Look below you," it said.

I had eyes but couldn't 'look' around. I floated up-ward and faced downward, and I saw through the tunnel, the man had left the room and Jackson was doing CPR on my lifeless body.

"Oh my God," I said.

"Don't worry, you'll go back to your body. We're not ready for you here yet. So, let's get the obvious questions out of the way," it said.

"Who are you?" I asked.

"That's pretty obviously the first question. I have many names, but you can call me Zeus," it said.

"Like the Greek God?" I asked.

"Where do you think they got that name? It didn't just appear out of nowhere," Zeus replied.

"I don't understand," I said.

"Alright Graham, I'll start. I'm an interdimensional being, in charge of your planet's evolution, both consciously, spiritually and in general. Most civilizations end up blowing themselves up once they figure out nuclear weaponry like what happened on Mars for example. But you have managed to not do that yet, though the temptation is irresistible. We have high hopes for Earth this time," Zeus said.

"Interdimensional, so where are you in our material dimension?" I asked.

"My lower self is somewhere in Cassiopeia as you refer to it," it said.

"This is crazy," I said. I looked down at Jackson again, and he was not giving up.

"Is it? In the 1930's your time, two separate scientists, Jansky and Reber, sent radio signals to Cassiopeia. Shortly thereafter they received my response. They were unable to decode it, as I coded it in the event someone evil got a hand on it. When they died, their work was confiscated by the government. Nobody has tried again since. But I'm here, waiting to help," Zeus said.

"I don't understand," I replied.

"Have you ever heard of the WOW signal?" He asked.

"Of course," I said.

"Then why is any of this a surprise to you?" Zeus asked.

"I don't know, this is a lot to handle right now," I said.

"Keep asking," he said.

I thought for a minute.

"What is our true history on this planet?" I asked.

"Very good, Graham. You're not going to like this answer, but it is the truth. Roughly 350,000 years your time, an alien race from Alpha Centuri had ruined their atmosphere and needed finely refined Gold to replace it. They had run out on their planet, so they went to the nearest solar system and found Earth. They came to Earth, and, when they got here, they saw primitive beings. They came here and tinkered with the DNA. You're familiar with Genesis 1:26 right?" He asked.

"And God said, let us make man in our image, after our likeness; and let them have dominion over the fish of the sea," I replied.

"Exactly. But the Bible has been mistranslated and misled. The Elohim is plural. It's not God. Also, 'God' said make man in OUR image. This implies multiple entities," he said.

"I don't understand," I said.

"It's a mistranslation. It's a very deep sentence actually, has multiple functions. Many people say that it's make man in our image, as in the creation of man, the story of Adam. But that's a misnomer. It's supposed to be read, 'make man in OUR IMAGE.' Man was already on Earth, they were just created in the image, as in, self-awareness, consciousness," he said. "Also, Man is the sign of Aquarius, and the fish in the sea is the sign of Pisces. It's a double entendre, that sentence," Zeus said.

"What happened next?" I asked.

"They came to Earth and tinkered with the DNA. The original plan for humans was that they would mine Gold for these entities. That was their entire plan. However, they eventually began to rebel. Not only that, but these entities would cross breed with the women. There are plenty of Bible verses talking about how they mated with the daughters of man," he said.

"Gold? We were created to mine gold?" I asked.

"Why do you think gold has ALWAYS been the most valuable commodity in the history of Earth? What is value? Who decided that this was currency? This CAME from somewhere Graham," Zeus said.

"I don't believe this," I said.

"There was a man named Albert Perry who got his DNA done at one of the Ancestry things that you humans have these days. His DNA test came back with an ancestor from 338,000 years ago. A good 100,000 years longer than any other human. Now how is this possible?" Zeus asked.

"I, I don't know," I said.

"Also, Rhesus negative blood isn't of your planet. The people with negative blood have alien DNA in them," he said.

"Well, I have read conspiracies about that?" I said.

"It's real, Graham," he said.

"Your geneticists already know that work has been done to your DNA, they just don't understand it, so nobody talks about it. Look at your second Chromosome. A close look at it shows a fray in it that looks like it was 'welded together or edited' so to speak. It's not even a debate about that. The second Chromosome was one of the first tinkering that was ever done to your species. It's about 8% of your total DNA. It was also done a little sloppily. Some of the most horrifying disorders on your planet are second Chromosome DNA anomalies. Autism, ALS, Epilepsy, Harlequin type ichthyosis, Lewy Body," he said.

I was silent.

"There's something called a Petradox on your planet, Graham. It's an electrical component left behind by an entity. It's buried in a stone. The stone is 100,000 years old. And these stories make the news, but it doesn't fit your narrative, so people ignore it. People gloss over the ancient stories of God's mythology and the names that came up. Like mine for instance! Haven't you ever read the Theogony of Hesiod?"

"No," I said.

"Well that's a shame. It's the first attempt at your planet putting stories together about how all the Gods came about," he said.

"How do you know all of this?" I asked.

"My higher self has access to the Akashic records. You've heard of that right?" He asked.

"Yes, I have. But how does that work?" I asked.

"Everything, every being on Earth began in the belly of the Star. The iron in your blood could only be forged in such. You have millions upon millions of particles in your body that came from the Earth before you. Every saying, every thought is recorded in this infinite record-keeping. You can't access it even here, but as your consciousness grows after death and you start ascending the dimensions, you will," he said.

"What now?" I asked.

"Do you have any other questions?" He asked.

"Can we travel through time?" I asked.

"That's being discovered on your planet right now. Some physicists have found a way to entangle particles together. It's complicated, but usually when hot and cold are placed together, hot energy goes to warm up cold.

They've found a way to draw heat from cold and add to hot. It's a start. Time travel doesn't work like you think it will work, but when you enter higher dimensions, time becomes plastic," he said.

"That sounds like something Jackson would say to me," I said.

"Speaking of which, I have to send you back now. If I wait much longer you won't be much use to yourself. Brace yourself, because this is really going to hurt. One last thing," he said.

"What's that?" I asked.

"You're not going to be able to remember any of this information I've told you," he said.

"What? Why?" I asked.

"It will be saved in your higher self, but your Earth mind won't have it," he said.

"Why?" I asked.

"Because it will ruin the rest of your life for you. Life is about discovery," Zeus finished.

"Even the part about our true past?" I asked.

"Especially that. It's there on Earth though. In the tablets of Enki. In the Emerald tablets of Thoth. This is literally the story that the Sumerians first left you. You've read the Flower of Life already though, which goes into it. You already knew this. You shouldn't be so surprised," Zeus said.

I suddenly felt a giant push in my solar plexus region, and all the wind knocked out of my body. I felt like I was diving into a freezing cold pool. Then suddenly I opened my eyes, and I felt a pain in my chest that I've never felt before.

Education isn't something you can finish

—*Isaac Asimov*

Chapter Eleven

"You ok bro?" Jackson asked. "It's so good to have you back. I was scared I lost you," he said.

It took me a minute to get my breathing in order. Very shallow breaths. I tried to stand up and winced and laid back down.

"Sorry bro, but I've been doing CPR on you for like three minutes," he said.

"Well, if you don't break some ribs, you're not doing it right," I said. I didn't think they were broken, but they sure as fuck were bruised. "Where's that asshole?" I asked.

"He left, but I was able to steal this from him," he said as he showed me a watch.

"How'd you get that?" I asked.

"When he put it down on the gurney after you died and checked on you, I put it in my pocket. He seemed disheveled. I didn't think he was planning on that killing you," Jackson said.

I sat there for a second and looked around the room. I was only out for three minutes?

"Also, I heard something. One of the men came into the room to check on him after this happened and I heard them talking about Genesis 32:30 on the way out. He said, 'if you ever need to get out of that situation, Genesis 32:30,' " he said.

I tried sitting up again, wincing in pain but finally did. The man had brought in some water. I reached over to the bottle and took a giant gulp of water. Aside from the pain, I feel completely refreshed. Like my blackout gave me the best sleep of my life. I felt the white light again, but I just can't remember anything. It was so much easier on DMT.

"What time is it?" I asked.

"1:45 in the morning," Jackson replied.

"Genesis 32:30. Hmmm," I said.

"Do you know the passage?" He asked.

"And Jacob called the name of the place Peniel: for I have seen God face to face, and my life is preserved," I said.

"What does that mean?" Jackson asked.

"I have no idea. Wait, you said they need this to leave this room?" I asked.

"That's what I overheard," he said.

"Jax," I began, "what do you say about getting out of here?" I asked.

"I'm fine with that," he said.

I sat for a minute and thought to myself about it. I continued to think about it until Jackson interrupted me.

"When you died," he began.

"Yeah?" I asked.

"Did you see anything?" He finished.

"I remember being immersed in an incredibly loving white light, but I don't remember anything besides that. I remember not wanting to come back," I said.

"Well, I'm glad you did, because this isn't how it ends for me. I will live to dream another day," he said.

I sat and thought about what he said, and a lightbulb went off in my head.

"Of course," I said.

"What?" He asked.

"Jax, you're a genius," I began. "Dreaming. Dreaming comes from DMT which is released through your pineal gland during sleep. It's the third eye. Jacob saw God, but it's not in Peniel, it's Pineal. The ancients must have known about this. Here, help me up," I said to him.

Jackson took a moment and slowly helped me to my feet, still wincing in pain from my bruised ribs. We walked over to the wall of carvings. I scanned it completely from top to bottom.

"There!" I said.

"There what?" He asked.

"The Freemasons have 33 degrees in their sect because of the 33 bones in the vertebrae. When you become a 33'rd, you've reached the top bone, which is settled deep within your brain by the Pineal Gland. When you're a 33rd degree, you have reached 'Christ Consciousness' metaphorically. The ancient Egyptians knew this as well. If you make a sagittal cut in the brain, it exposes the pineal gland," I said.

"And?" He asked.

"And, it looks EXACTLY like something," I said scanning the wall.

"Like what?" He asked.

"Like THAT," I said as I pointed to the ancient Egyptian Eye of Horus directly in front of us.

"Now what?" He asked.

"You heard what he told the man about leaving," I said as I pushed the panel containing the depiction of the Eye of Horus. A panel opened up, and there was a new engravement on a small keypad. I quickly shut the panel and had Jackson help me back to the cot.

"What are you two doing?" The man asked.

"Nothing," I said.

"Good," he said as he left. As soon as he left, I turned to Jackson.

"That's our way out," I said.

Jackson checked his watch, it was 2:45.

"We're about to get half an hour uninterrupted time in about fifteen minutes," he said.

"Good., I said as I laid back down.

Day 6 3AM

"Get up, let's do this thing," Jackson said and hoisted me up. Sometimes I can't get over how strong this guy is.

We hobbled over to the panel and pushed it open again. We saw a keypad with some words carved above it. Next to the keypad we saw a tube that ran down into a tank labeled Tabun.

"Oh shit," I said.

"What?" He said.

"We've got one shot at this. This sensor is hooked up to a tank of Tabun nerve gas. It was discovered in 1936, but rarely used. Very lethal. It's going to seep through the vents in the floor and kill us," I said.

He nodded at me, and we went back to looking at the words engraved into the panel.

Matthew 7:9-11 Which of you, if your son asks for bread, will give him a stone? Find Simon.

I couldn't believe what I was reading in front of my very eyes. I had given an entire lecture about Matthew a little while back that I wrote about in my latest book, but I don't recall this piece. Find Simon? I slowly sunk down to the floor and sat there trying to figure things out.

"Does that make any sense to you?" Jackson asked.

"A little," I replied. "The bread is the wheat stalk held by Virgo, so that's the eighth sign. I know this. Also, the most important signs, a sign can know is its neighboring sign, or its cross sign. Neighbors are Leo and Libra 7,9, and it's cross sign is 2, Pisces," I said.

"How do we know which one that is?" He asked.

"I'm not really sure right now, just let me think for a minute," I said.

"We've got twenty minutes until someone comes back and they check on us." I almost died last time, I don't think my body can handle it again. Shit.

I sat there on the floor tracing the Zodiac with my hands in the air and trying to figure this out. Simon? The disciple? How does he have anything to do with this. Then it occurred to me out of nowhere, that each disciple has to represent a specific sign of the Zodiac. 12 disciples, 12 signs. But which one was Simon?

"Fifteen minutes," Jackson said.

I started to get a little nervous. This was our only chance out of here, and I was stumped. Plus, I'm conditioned to get nervous when Jackson counts down time, like he did in that spiked pit of hell in Jerusalem.

"Come on Graham. I don't know why the most complicated things I've seen since I've been with Rosette have been with these ancient Jews. ten minutes," he said.

I sat there and smiled for a minute at the thought of what he said, and then it hit me.

"Simon is Peter," I said.

"So?" He asked.

"But why?" I asked.

"I don't know. It doesn't make any sense," he said.

"It does, if you know your Astrology," I said as I stood up. "So why Peter? We already know that it's either 2,7 or 9. But do you know what the ruling planet of Pisces is? Pisces, the time period of Jesus?" I asked.

"Not sure," he said.

"It's Neptune. Actually, technically it is Jupiter. You said it before, these ancient Jews. Jupiter, or JewPeter. That's why Simon is sometimes called Peter. Peter is the rock that Jesus builds his Church on. The bread is Virgo. The code is 28," I said.

"Are you sure? If you're wrong, we're going to die," he said.

"If we don't put it in, we're going to die," I said.

"Fair enough," he said as he punched the code in.

We heard a beeping then saw a bright flash of light emit from it. Suddenly to our right, a small door opened. We looked at each other, closed the panel, then walked towards it. We both entered the tunnel and shut the door behind us.

"We've still got eight minutes before they get back and notice we're gone. Let's get the fucking fuck out of here," Jackson said.

"I'm with you bud," I said.

Jackson helped carry me down the path, which we walked/jogged. After about a five-minute run, we ended up at a door.

"Let's see what's outside, shall we?" I asked.

We opened the door, and it lead to the outside world. Sweet buttery Jesus, freedom! We walked outside, then Jackson put his arm back and held me back. There was a guard with a gun patrolling outside.

"Wait here bro," Jackson said.

He carefully crouched and ran up to the man and put him in a rear naked choke. The man quickly passed out. Jackson took his keys and gun and came back to me. We started walking to our right, when we saw a small building, that was attached to where we initially came in. At least, it must have been I thought. Jackson and I walked to it and opened the door.

There was a man playing solitare, not really paying attention to the camera screens around him. Jackson slowly walked up to him and pointed the gun at him. The guard put his hands up and turned around. Jackson put him on his knees and then slammed him in the back of the head with the gun. The man hit the ground like a sack of potatoes. Then Jackson started looking through the man's desk. Surprising to both of us, he found our cell phones, batteries and SIM cards. He reassembled them and turned his phone on.

In the corner of my eye I saw a plastic bag in the corner of the room that said 'dispose.' I went to it curiously and opened it up. It was our clothes from a week ago. I snapped my fingers at Jackson, and he saw. He ran over to me with the phone, and we got out of our clothes and back into our street clothes. Good riddance. If I never see another pair of white anything again, it would be too soon. Jackson finally got his phone on, and he immediately received a call.

"Hello?" He answered as he put the phone on speaker.

"Oh my God baby, you're alive. I was so worried about you, we all thought that you were dead, and I'm just so grateful that you're still here, I'm going to cry, but oh, wait, hold on," Rosette said as she handed the phone over to Larisa.

"You guys had us fucking scared. I tagged your SIM cards so that if they were used to turn another phone on, I could ping you and get your location. Where the fuck are you?" Larisa said.

"I literally have no idea," Jackson said. "I'm standing here with Graham, and we've just been tortured for a week, I'm starving, and I knocked these guards out, I have their gun, we just got our clothes back . . ." She cut him off.

"Alright sit tight, I'm triangulating your cell from the nearby towers to get an exact point. I'll send you an uber there," Larisa said. "Wait, did you say you got your clothes back?" She asked.

"Don't ask Larisa," he said.

"Alright that's fine, listen, things might be a little scary when you get out there incidentally," she said.

"Why's that?" He questioned back.

"In the week you've been gone, this virus has done a lot of damage. It's basically carnage in every major city in the North. It hasn't hit the rural areas yet, which we're trying to figure out why. Fuck, I won't bore you with the details. You're looking for a white Explorer, should be there in five minutes," she said.

"Does it have to be white?" He winced back.

"I don't understand," she replied

"We'll explain everything when we see you. Where the hell are we by the way?" He asked.

"You're at an abandoned mental institution in Connecticut. Jean paid the uber off and left him a nice tip, he's going to bring you back to us. I'm going to go in case somebody tripped this call," she said and hung up.

Jackson looked over to me. "They should be getting back now."

"I know," I said as I walked over to him.

We sat in the room for a few minutes, the uber came early. Jackson helped me to the car. Just as we got in and drove away, I looked back and saw a team of men entering where we came out, guns drawn. We had escaped death for now, but the experience was going to stay with us for a long time.

Chapter Twelve

"Dr. Spear, they escaped," Dr. Rorja said.

"What?!" He replied incredulously. "How?" He asked.

"They cracked the failsafe code to leave the room. They also took out two guards and were last seen running to a car and then speeding off," he said.

Dr. Spear paced around the room frantically, finally kicking his chair. That got everybody perked up.

"I HATE the fact that we are tied down to this Bible based bullshit," Dr. Spear said.

Everybody was silent. What he just said was cause for much concern. He sat there for a minute in his chair and had a quizzical look on his face. Finally, he started to smile.

"It doesn't even matter," he began. "It's too late for them to stop it. People are dying all over the World right now because of this. They don't matter at this point anymore," he said.

"What's our next move?" Dr. Dotpun asked.

"We are going to sit here and wait for this to go viral," he said as he smiled to himself. "See what I did there with that word," he laughed to himself.

"Maybe we've taken this thing too far," Dr. Rorja said.

"Doctor," Spear began, "I'm aware you have just lost your two eldest sons. But they knew the rules and knew what they were getting into when they made those choices. Please know, that had it been my daughter that had done what they did, I would have done the same thing. You already know you are going to see them again on a different frequency after you leave Earth. Try not to think about it too much," Dr. Spear said.

"I don't think that's much to console me Doctor," Dr. Rorja said.

They sat around the table and discussed their next big plans. About where they would live when this outbreak hits critical mass, about how they would eventually find a 'cure' to it and charge people an arm and a leg to rid themselves of this horrible thing they've concocted. But something didn't sit right with Dr. Rorja. His alliance to his sons was pressing on his mind. If there was one chance to right this ship, he was going to have to give up everything. His billions, possibly his youngest son Logan, who was still alive. He was going to have to give up his wife, that married into his family. All elite families interbreed to keep their money together, and her being from the wealthy Frecklerole family, they would never allow them to remain together if they discover what he was planning on doing. It became more clear to him as this meeting continued, that these men didn't give a fuck about anything. They didn't have a soul, all they cared about was power and wealth. Him losing his two children for trying to help save humanity was weighing on him. He decided to himself right then and there that he wanted to be on the right side of history. He will continue to be part of the meetings, but he will reach out to Graham Newsdon and help them get to the bottom of this. If there was one person on this planet that had disrupted the global powers more in the last two and a half years, it was the kid who lost his brother in that accident. He had to reach out to him, but he wasn't going to be able to leave Switzerland, otherwise they would assume that he went to help them. He was assured by Dr. Spear that they went quick and painless, and he wondered if his fate would be the same. True bravery comes in the form of standing up for what's right, in the face of people trying to take your life. The only questions would be, how would he meet with Graham, and what are the chances that he would be trusted after all the shit that he probably heard about him?

I am not one who was born in the possession of knowledge. I am one who is fond of antiquity and earnest in seeking it there —Confucius

Education is an admirable thing. But it is well to remember from time to time that nothing that is worth knowing can be taught —Oscar Wilde

Chapter Thirteen

We pulled up to the house at a little past 4:00 a.m. We tipped the uber driver an additional fifty dollars for his generous ride back home for us. Everything was pitch black outside, as had been the entire trip home. I opened the door, disabled the trip wire and ran upstairs past everyone and into my room. I fumbled around the drawers until I found my 'Spice grinder' and pulled out a shroom cap. I shoved it in there and ground it to a powder. I rolled up a dollar bill and went to inhale it, but then I remembered you can't take it that way. This wasn't going to be fast enough. Finally, Jackson came around the corner with a worried Hannah.

"Um babe, thanks for saying hi," Hannah said annoyed.

"Just, give me a minute," I said.

"What are you doing bro, you know you can't snort that," Jackson said.

"Shrooms I can't, but ah here it is," I said as I pulled out a little baggie.

"Is that cocaine?" Hannah asked alarmed.

"No, it's 4aco dmt. It's the same thing as psilocybin," I said as I measured out 0.3g. I had been dosing with 0.1g before, but I had just been through hell and back. I grabbed my dollar bill and took up the two lines that I cut for myself. It stung my nostrils, and I definitely got a sour postnasal drip. I walked backwards a few feet and sat on the bed with my hands on my head. Then I looked up. COLORS. I hadn't seen them in so long. You have no idea how you miss them until you're forced to live without them for nearly a week. Everybody came into the room.

"You OK Newsdon?" Rosette asked worriedly.

After about two minutes, I started to feel better. A little numb, but happier. See SSRI's increase the serotonin in your brain, but psychadelics mimick serotonin. I could feel my 5-HT2A receptor being triggered. After a few more seconds, I felt my BDNF being produced. I felt the Glutamate increase. I felt alive, well, slightly sedated but great. It's beyond me why this isn't legal yet. Oh wait, there's too much profit in big pharma. I could feel the dopamine levels increase in my brain. This dose wasn't high enough to cause hallucinations, but the colors were definitely more sharp. Or maybe that's because I hadn't seen them in so long.

I led everybody into the living room and sat down on the chair and turned to the TV. Blur was on. Apparently there were suicide pockets in South Africa, China, the Phillipines, Vietnam, Florida and Pennsylvania just to name a few places. This was indeed the beginning of Revelations. We were running out of time and had no clues.

"I was told on the train before we were captured, to look back at the flash drive. So first, thank you Larisa for finding us and getting us out of there. But I need you now more than ever," I said.

"We're just glad you're OK, mon ami," Jean said.

"OK, it's open. Now what are we looking for?" Larisa asked.

Take the fear out of the age of the people with no written history. Brothers till the end of time. Eye see DDC in the brothers. It's the poison within. Find the cure.

"Who on this planet has no written history?" I asked.

"Maybe it's not a who, but a when," Hannah responded.

I was a little fuzzy still, but I started thinking about it. Maybe it's my newfound self-medicating experimenting that I was on, but it hit me like a ton of bricks.

"OK, so we have the Christians in Pisces, the Jews in Aries, the Egyptians in Taurus, even the Sumerians were in Taurus. But there's no written history for Gemini. The twins. Brothers until the end of time," I said.

"Brilliant Graham, but that's not the whole thing," Hannah said.

"I know, just, just give me a minute to think," I said, rubbing my eyes. It was nearly 5:00 a.m. at this point, and I haven't had a decent night of sleep without screaming being pumped into my earholes.

"The Medusa Nebula is in Gemini. When you see her eye, you turn to stone. Find the poison within that? Wait, that can't be right. Also, how is something in Gemini going to help us getting people to stop killing themselves here?" I asked.

"Keep looking. Rosette? Larisa? Do you ladies have anything?" Hannah asked.

"Nothing yet," Larisa said as she scanned the computer screen back and forth like a tennis match.

"Baby, we're all exhausted, let's just go to bed and figure this out in the morning," Jean said to Larisa.

"I think I may have something Graham," Larisa said.

"Well what is it? I asked?

"Eye see DDC in the brothers. DDC isn't code for anything that I'm aware of," she said.

"Where are you going with this?" Jackson asked, now he was rubbing his eyes too.

"What if it's another code, like the code I decoded before. What if DDC is English gematria. What if it's 443?" She asked.

"So, what if it is, what does that mean for us?" Hannah asked.

"What if eye see is IC. It's just phonetic. If you combine these two, you get IC 443. Graham, do you know what this is?" Larisa asked.

"Jesus, I can't believe I didn't see it before," I said. "It's the name for the jellyfish Nebula in Gemini. But what's the poison within? What do we know about jellyfish?" I asked. It had occurred to me that one of the last things Frances said was that the new order would have to do with Gemini.

"They can clone themselves," Hannah said.

"They have evolved for 650 million years and don't have brains," Jackson added.

"Some glow in the dark," Larisa included.

"The Scarlet Jellyfish is basically immortal," I said.

"What about that jellyfish that they just found, the warty comb jellyfish that only has an asshole when it poops, then it just vanishes," Jackson said.

"Shit though, none of this is helping. What is it about the jellyfish?" I asked.

"This entire thing is PISSING ME OFF. I want to go back to that hellhole with a bat and just beat the living hell out of everyone there at that torture prison camp," Jackson hollered.

"Confucius say, the louder the monkey, the smaller its balls. Let's just try and calm down sweetie," Rosette said.

That got a chuckle out of me. I can't believe I almost forgot how to laugh. Why is it always us that has to go through this stuff. Why can't I just sit at home and play Mario Kart with my friends and just ignore the world. Suddenly my What's App rang on my phone. This can't be good. I looked at my phone for a few seconds at this unknown number.

"Are you going to pick it up?" Jackson asked.

"If they wanted to track it, they wouldn't need him. Anyway, it might be too late," Hannah said.

"Actually, it's What's App. It's got a shitty security system, but it's hard to crack in and hear the conversation. He should be fine," Larisa said as she nodded to me to pick up.

"Hello?" I asked.

"Don't hang up, just give me ninety seconds of your time," the voice on the other end of the line said.

"Who is this? How did you get my number?" I asked.

"We don't have time for that, you're asking the wrong questions," the voice said.

"What question should I be asking?" I asked.

"Put me on speakerphone," the voice said.

I complied. At this point I didn't know if I was hallucinating this entire conversation, or if I was actually still asleep at the facility.

"You received the flash drive, yes?" The voice said.

"Look, if you think you can intimidate us," Jackson said before he was cut off.

"I'm not interested in wasting anybody's time. The truth is, the only time that might be running out is mine for reaching out to you," the voice said.

"Who exactly are you?" I asked.

"The two boys that met you in Boston and New York, they were my sons," the voice said.

It was then that it occurred to me that I was speaking to a very powerful head of a family, Dr. Rorja.

"I'm sorry for your loss Dr. Rorja. You must know that we had nothing to do with that," I said.

"I'm aware of that. To be honest, ever since you escaped, you haven't been deemed much of a threat anymore. Now that the sickness is spreading to other countries, it might be too late for you to do something about it. The council has decided to leave you alone," he said.

I sat there for a minute bewildered at how a few years ago I was in a frat playing drinking games, and now my life was being debated by the most secretive powerful families in the world. To be honest, it's a miracle that we only lost NP, and that we are all still here. I know, famous last words, right?

"What do you want from us?" I asked.

"I was going to have you come to Basel to meet me so I can fill you in on everything that's happened, but I think by the time you get to me and get back, the sickness will have spread to all continents. The flash drive. Was there a picture on it?" Dr. Rorja asked.

"Yes, there was, why?" Larisa replied.

"What was it?" He asked.

"A picture of Jesus against the Sun," Larisa said.

Dr. Rorja chuckled to himself. "Well, at least my son had a sense of humor about him. Young miss?" He reached out.

"Yes," Larisa replied.

"Are you absolutely certain that there is nothing out of the ordinary with that picture?" He asked.

"Well, it never occurred to me to look deeper into it, hold on a moment please," she said.

While she worked, I pepped Dr. Rorja with some more questions.

"So, we're safe, but you're not," I asked.

"My dear child, nobody is safe anymore. My sons are gone, and, although I know I'll see them again in another dimension outside of space and time, the pain is too great right now. I'm giving you this help because I feel that my time is coming to an end, and for once, it would be nice to have my name attached to something positive," he said.

"Got something," Larisa said.

"What?" I asked.

"It was embedded. It's called Steganography. See, on the surface level, you only see the picture, but it can be used to store a ton of zip files within it. This file that I found only has one, but it's password encrypted," she said.

"Any idea Doctor?" I asked.

"IC443," he said.

Larisa typed it in, and the file opened up.

"Um Graham, you might want to come take a look at this," she said.

"What is it?" I asked.

"It's information on R&D from Bionic," she said.

I froze. I thought back to when Jackson and I were literally in front of Bionic, and Emile kept looking at the building and smirking and shaking his head. He had led us there all along. It had only cost him his life.

"What else does it say?" Dr. Rorja asked from the phone.

"It says that they had been endowed their net worth through shell corporations and offshore accounts in order to come up with a very specific 'antigen' that could be used for 'military purposes,'" she said.

"What can we do about this?" I asked.

"Hold on, I'm trying to get the map layout of it," she said.

We sat there for a moment until she spoke up.

"I've got the blueprints for this place. We'll go over it together shortly. I'm going to try and get into their system right now," she said.

"I'd be very careful. They have a top-notch security system," Dr. Rorja said. "You don't think they were selected by accident, do you?" He asked.

We waited for another minute or two until she spoke up again.

"OK, so the first level is GUI based," she said.

"Is that like an STD for computers?" Rosette joked.

"No girl, GUI like gooey. It's graphic user interface. Like what you're used to on your computer. Only it's just a picture," she said.

"What's the picture of?" Jackson asked.

"It's a seashell in an array of colors in Fibonacci sequence. I'm sorry, but I don't know what I have to do here, I need to call up an old friend," Larisa said.

She pulled out her phone and dialed Phil. He was her mentor at MIT and remained close with her.

"Hello?" A sleepy voice on the other end of the phone said.

"Phil, it's Riss. I NEED a favor from you," she said.

"Do you know what time it is?" He asked.

"Yes, you know I wouldn't call unless it was work or life and death related," she said.

"Well which one is it?" His voice peppered up.

"Technically work. I'm trying to worm into a security system, and I've got this GUI image. There's no password or anything that I can enter," she said.

"Riss, what's the image?" He asked.

She told him.

"Larisa, it's a fractal image," he said. "For this type of security, you need to zoom in and find the discrepancy. You should be able to backdoor in at that point," he said.

"YES, of course! Thanks a million Phil. Talk to you later," she said.

"Let me know how it goes," he said and hung up.

She hung up the phone and went furiously back to work. After a few minutes her eyes lit up, followed by a look of horror on her face. She shut her laptop.

"So, I wormed in, but that was just the first level of security. There's a much tougher level that I need to get through, but there's a Mesh network of floaters monitoring it," she said.

"In English?" I asked.

"Sorry, this is a serious security system and the only way I'm going to be able to get in is if I Ghost it," she said.

"So, Ghost it," Rosette said.

"Not so simple beautiful," she began, "I need to hook in directly to the security system. Which, from the looks of these plans, is in the basement. We'll have to go tomorrow and do some recon at Bionic, then go back home, get ready and go at night," she said.

"If there's no other way, I guess we should just go to bed now," I said. It's not as if millions of peoples lives were depending on us or anything.

"Probably a wise idea children. Have a good night, I hope I don't have to talk to you again," Dr. Rorja said as he hung up.

We went to bed and I passed out nearly immediately. Tomorrow was going to be a long day. Little did we know that I would lose the most precious thing I have in my life by the end of the day.

Religion is the impotence of the human mind to deal with occurrences it cannot understand. —Karl Marx.

Without deviation from the norm, progress is not possible —Frank Zappa

Chapter Fourteen

We woke up around 9:00. We all took turns showering and getting dressed. Today was going to be a crazy day. Once we all got dressed, we went down the block to the Diner to have breakfast and go over our plans for the day.

"OK, so what is the first thing we need to do today?" I asked.

"Well, mon ami, I am going to go with Larisa to pick up an unmarked van so we can all travel together," Jean said.

"Good call," Rosette said.

"I agree," I said.

"But what then?" Jackson asked.

I was distracted because I was watching another AquaStream video of a preacher who was getting a lot of attention lately, trying to disprove me. Rosette could see that I was getting upset, and she took my phone.

"Graham, listen to me," she said.

She never calls me Graham. I perked right up.

"What you've done online with your following is destroy the previous confirmation bias of many people. The shit you talk about isn't something that fits neatly into their paradigms and they're lashing out. There are those out there who fall to the Barnum effect of Astrology, who you've given a deeper and more lasting understanding of what it truly is. When you got your information out there in front of the world, you created the Baader-Meinhof phenomenon. For every preacher that's out there trying to destroy your work, there's a kid who's seeing the signs of Astrotheology wherever he goes. At the same time, these preachers when they hear you, it only causes the backfire effect. They double down on their beliefs. You need to stop worrying about what everybody thinks, and just do you," she finished.

Typical psychological rant by Rosette. But very useful. It did calm me down a little bit. "OK Rosette, you're right. I'm going to put this out of my mind. We've got a lot to do today. OK, so we get the Van, then what?" I asked.

"Then, we go to Bionic, and you and Jackson go in and do some recon for the place. Remember, I can't disable the alarm system unless I can plug directly into the computer. When I get home, I'll pull up the layout of the building. I should be able to get into City Hall's record vault online," Larisa said.

"OK great, so you ready for this Jackson?" I asked.

"Of course, Graham. After what we've been through, we're quantum entangled now," he said.

"Did you know that in 1634 Catholic monks invented the all beer lent diet that they called 'liquid bread,' " I said. As usual, when Graham goes physics, I go silly.

"Is that true?" Jean asked.

"Don't humor him," Rosette said.

We paid for breakfast and headed home. Jean and Larisa went to rent a van, and we just sat around for an hour waiting for them to get back.

"Jackson, what are you writing about this time?" Hannah asked.

"Do you ever wonder why gravity is weaker than the other three forces?" He asked.

"Oh God, not again," I said.

"Seriously. It just doesn't make sense. I've been reading up on the possibility of a fifth underlying force. One that connects all of them together. I'm just jotting down some notes," he said.

I sat there and watched TV. My mind led me back to my room, and I considered microdosing again. Except for the fact that I read that if you do it every day, it has less of an effect on you, and I basically tripled my dose the day before. I should probably lay off it for a while. I had a bit of the shakes, but that was because of that night they made me drink the whole bottle. I had gone so long without a drop, now I feel like I was pulled right back into it. I did have a great support group that would never let me fall back into it though. I pushed that thought out of my head. Finally, Larisa and Jean returned.

"OK guys, we have the van. Here, Jax and Graham. I picked these up for you," Larisa said as she tossed us two lab coats and doctors masks.

"How are we going to get in the building?" I asked.

"The building is open during the day. After 5:00 it requires a pass. I'll work on that once we get the info we need," she said as she opened her computer and started doing her thing.

"What exactly are we looking for when we get in there?" I asked.

"OK, so here's the layout of the place. I ripped it from Town Hall. Their security is child's play," Larisa said. "OK, so here is R&D, that's where you need to go. When you go in the building go to the elevator, take it to the third floor, turn left, cross the bridge, and it will be on the other side. I need to go in the basement. That's where all the servers are being held in a key coded room. It's a five-digit alphanumeric code, and my algorithm should be able to break it, but I'll need ten minutes uninterrupted," she said.

"Right, but what exactly are we looking for?" I asked.

"You'll know when you see it," Larisa said.

"What are we going to do in the meanwhile?" Rosette asked.

"You, Hannah and my horny hubby are going to wait in the van for us. If anything goes sour, I'll message you through my computer and you take off. We'll park in the garage of this place," Larisa said.

"I like a girl that takes charge," Jean said.

"Slow down cowboy," Larisa said and winked to him.

I rolled my eyes. These two jack rabbits are what I'm pinning my faith on. I turned to Jackson and nodded. We went into the room and changed into our outfits. We came back out.

"You look so good baby," Rosette said as her pupils dilated. Between Jean, Larisa and Rosette I wouldn't be surprised if this broke out into an orgy before we left.

"Can we get a move on here?" I asked.

"Good idea," Larisa said as she closed her laptop.

We made our way down the stairs, disabled the trip alarm, and closed the door behind us. We piled into the van. My heart started beating in my throat. How was I more nervous about this than I was when we were being tortured?

Philosophy is really homesickness

—*George MacDonald*

Chapter Fifteen

We pulled up at Bionic and went into the garage.

"OK, guys, let's do this thing," Larisa said.

The three of us got out of the car and went towards the building. We were all wearing masks, which was a common occurrence around this area as many were dealing with live virals. We sat and talked outside, then followed a busy looking man into the building. We went to the elevator, and I pressed the up and down button. The elevator going down came first.

"OK guys, I'll see you on the other side," Larisa said as she went in and pushed the button for the basement. She disappeared behind the closing doors. Then, right on cue, the elevator heading upstairs came. We got in and pressed three.

"You OK Graham, you're sweating and shaking a little bit," Jackson said.

"It's from the alcohol the other night. I'll be fine, I just need to shake it off," I said. I was considering going home and taking a Valium after all this. Hopefully a good night's rest will allow me to reset my biology.

Unfortunately for me, sleep isn't something that was built into my life anymore.

The elevator came to a jolt on the third floor. We got out and followed Larisa's directions. Everything was exactly as she described. Fuck, she's good, I thought to myself. We made our way to R&D, but when we got there I frowned. There was a thumbprint scan to get into the room. Jackson and I sat outside the door for a while talking, until finally two people came out. They were on their way to lunch and engrossed in that. We slipped in the room.

The first thing I noticed was that there was an Iphone X in a cage. I spent a minute looking at it. I took out my watch and snapped a picture of it and sent it to Larisa with a question mark. We looked around the room and it was a typical lab setting. Centrifuges and vials everywhere, everything neatly labeled, everything has a place. There were a few other people in the room with us, maybe four that were engrossed in what they were doing. My watch vibrated with a message back from Larisa.

What does the phone say on it?

I walked back over to the phone and took a close look at it. It had the temperature in the room. It also had some kind of measuring device sticking out the side of it. I texted Larisa back.

"Jax, let's go," I said.

"Not until we get what we came for," he said.

"What did we come for exactly?" I asked.

"That!" He said as he pointed to the back of the room. It was where they kept all their samples. We walked up to the area and looked inside. Just then I got a text from Larisa to my phone.

That's a temperature gauge. When everybody leaves, the room is set at a specific temperature. If a person enters the room his body emits heat. If the temperature goes up one degree, an alarm is triggered. Wait, what kind of phone was that again?

The newest Iphone. I texted her back.

We were in the room with all the samples. Suddenly we heard a voice.

"Hey! You're not supposed to be in there. Who are you?" The person asked.

"I'm sorry, we were just looking for my phone," I said as I picked it up off the counter.

"You know you're not supposed to have phones in here. They get locked in the bin," the man said.

"I'm sorry, I forgot, we're heading out," I said. Jackson and I walked out of the room, but out of the corner of my eye I caught something. One of the vials in black marker was marked IC443. That HAD to be it.

Jackson and I left R&D and walked around for a bit. Larisa was still working downstairs, so we went to the cafeteria to grab a bite to eat.

"Did you see that vial?" I asked Jackson.

"Yup, we'll have to come back and grab it when nobody's around late tonight," he said in between bites of his burger. Just then we got a text from Larisa.

I've got it, meet me at the van in five minutes

We quickly finished eating, then made our way outside. We got to the Van and we all settled in.

"Alright, it was tight, I had to hide between two stacks of servers. The heat generated from them was giving me hot flashes," she said.

"We found what we needed. But what are we supposed to do about the fingerprint to get in or the temperature gauge," I asked.

"I'll take care of those. Drive Rosette," Larisa said.

"Aye aye captain," Rosette said.

"Jean, I'll need you to come with me. I have to pick up a few things," she said.

"Absolutement," he said. "What exactly do we need to get?"

"I'll explain once we have them and we get back to the house."

We got back to the house and Jean and Larisa got into their car and sped off. We sat upstairs and thought about what he had just been through. What exactly was in that vial. How are we going to get in that locked building, and how are we going to not set the sensor off. We turned on the TV again.

European countries are facing mass suicides all across France, Spain, the UK. Johannesburg was hit as well. It might be a little too early to say, but this might be how our World ends. The WHO has no information for us, and the UN has been silent. How much more of this can we endure?

I watched this anchor lose their shit on the TV. Then something occurred to me.

"Hey guys, how come it's only developing nations that are being hit?" I asked.

"What do you mean, baby?" Hannah asked.

"Jo-berg was hit, but no news on the rest of South Africa. Europe was hit, but no news on most of South America. Even in the States, it's only the most populous areas that are hit. If this was something in the water or the vaccine, wouldn't we be able to narrow it down by now?" I asked.

"I don't think anybody has the answer to that," Jackson said. "But it is an interesting pattern," he finished.

I sat back in my chair and thought about the email that the nearly deceased Lilac Northinly gave me. Was that the President's personal email or was it just hers. Maybe I could email the president and tell him what I think I've figured out. I put that thought in my back pocket and lit up a cigarette. Seems to be the only thing that can calm me down these days.

2 hours later

"OK guys, so sit tight because I have to go over a few things with you," Larisa said as she and Jean came back in the house with a bunch of shit.

"What is all that?" I asked.

"Let me explain," she began. "This is a rubber 3D printed master thumbprint that I created at home. This should get you into the building and get you into the room and the rooms with the vials," she said.

"What's a master print?" Rosette asked.

"It's like a skeleton key, but for thumbprints," Larisa said.

"Wow," I said.

"OK next, you mentioned the Iphone that was checking the temperature. So, there's no way for you to go into the room and disable it without making it go off," she began, "however, I think I found another way," she said.

"What would that be?" I asked.

"For some reason, Iphones are incredibly sensitive to Helium. If you flood the phone with helium, it will disable it. It should give you about 15-20 minutes before it comes back on," she said.

"OK, so how are we supposed to do that?" Jackson asked.

"Well," Larisa began nervously, "So, here is a map of the duct system in the building. Graham, you're going to enter like you always do and take the elevator to the third floor, and there is a vent right when you walk out. You'll take the helium tank and the nozzle and follow this map that I've made for you, and when you get to the vent in the room, just turn the tank on and aim it at the phone. It will beep when it goes off, and then you can enter the room and let Jackson in," she said. "Oh, incidentally, you'll be doing this in pitch black," she said.

"Are you for real?" I asked.

"Don't worry, I stole a thing of night vision eye drops when the CIA came to recruit me at MIT," she said.

"What now?" Jean asked.

"You put these drops in your eyes, and it gives you temporary night vision. It dilates your pupils, and does a few other things, not important. But you should both be able to find your way around in the dark after I disable the main security and forward all the phones to voicemail. The backup security will still be on, hence why you need the thumbprint," Larisa said.

"Are you sure this is going to work?" I asked.

"It's our only real shot at this, so you better hope it does," Larisa said.

"OK, so we'll sit and wait for nighttime, and then we'll go," I said.

"Exactly," she replied.

We sat and watched TV. More countries were reporting mass suicides. Australia, Norway, Sweden, Japan. This shit has jumped to islands now. We looked at the map that the News had provided, and we could see that much of China, North and South Africa, remained very low in their suicide count. Why would these terrorists be targeting first world countries when all they've ever done is complain about third world countries? What in the living fuck was going on here?

Shortly, the public will be unable to reason or think for themselves. They'll only be able to parrot the information they've been given on the previous night's news.
—Zbiigniew Brzezinski

Chapter Sixteen

We left the house at a quarter to nine. We piled into the van and made our way on the 45-minute trip to Bionic. We arrived at Bionic right on time and coziest our van into the dark corner of the parking garage.

"OK guys, so first and foremost, lift your shirts up," Larisa said.

"Some late-night fun?" Jean asked. You could tell he had just a tinge of jealousy in him. I'd never seen him act this way around a girl before.

"No, you jackass, just do it," she said as she pulled out a water bottle with a spray.

We lifted our shirts, and she sprayed our chest and back with it.

"OK, guys, put your shirts down," she said.

"What was the point of that?" I asked.

"It's called smartdust. It was made by Hitachi. You can't see them, but there are a bunch of micro gps navigational dots on you. They are smaller than an eyelash, but should something happen to you guys again, I'll be able to track you down," Larisa said.

"How did you get a hold of this?" Jackson asked.

"I was recruited for the CIA remember?" She replied and winked.

"Anything else you stole that you want to let us know about?" I asked.

"No, I don't think so. But quiet, I need to get to work here," she said.

We talked for a little while about what we were looking for. I turned the radio on to hear the latest projections. The suicides have hit Houston, San Diego, Hawaii, since we've left the house. Estimated total dead, 200,000. We still aren't 100% sure what we're looking for, or where we'll be able to locate it. This was a hail mary against the wind right now.

"Dammit, this is a security system like I've never seen before," Larisa said.

"Why is it so difficult. Aren't you supposed to be like some kind of savant?" Rosette asked.

"I'm not a savant, I'm Larisa. Nice to meet you," she said and winked over to Rosette. Rosette giggled.

"What exactly is so complicated about this?" I asked.

"The security system is running code, but it's two running lines of code intertwined like a DNA Helix. If only I could find the primer in this, I would be able to . . ." She trailed off.

"You'd be able to what?" I asked.

"I think I have something here," she said and turned her computer around.

She faced the computer at us, and none of us could decipher what was going on. To me it looked like the running Matrix screen from the movie.

"See here's the thing. These are using exponentially high prime numbers circling around each other," she said.

"You can recognize a super prime?" I asked.

"Not the whole thing, but sequences of numbers I can. I just need to find the break in this," she replied.

"Aren't we going to get caught trying to break the system here?" Hannah asked.

"No, we'll be fine. I cloned my IP. They'll kick down a chicken butcher's door in Cambodia before they find me." She smiled and went back to work.

We sat there for about ten minutes while she worked.

"Why supreme prime numbers?" I asked.

"It's how the military does their security system. The Pentagon's security system is based on exponential prime number algorithms. Turns out prime numbers are very unpredictable at that level. I had to memorize the first 50 when I was at MIT, and I recognize some of them intertwined with each other in this helix. This security system is very fucking fresh. Like, must have just been installed recently," she said.

"Recently, like when all the problems started happening?" I asked.

"I'd bet my money on it," she said.

We let her work for a few more minutes, and then finally she jumped up out of her seat.

"I've got something," she said.

"What is it?" I asked.

"There's a break in the code where you can enter an override. Shit," she said.

"What?" Jackson asked.

"There's a riddle," she said.

"Tell us!" Rosette yelped.

"Protected by the greatest numbers in existence, so shall its downfall be the inverse," she said.

"Oh, come on!" I said.

"Crap," Hannah said.

"OK, no need to panic guys, we do this kind of shit all the time," I said.

"Its downfall shall be the inverse? What's the smallest number we know?" Hannah asked.

We sat for a few minutes deliberating over what we thought it could be. Nobody was coming up with any good answer until Jackson asked the pivotal question.

"How many characters is it?" He asked.

"Um, let's see. It looks like it's eight," Larisa said.

Jackson started rocking back and forth in the van and closed his eyes. He exhibits semi-autistic behavior when he's deep in thought. After a few minutes, he sprung up.

"I think I know what it is," he said.

"Well what is it?" I asked.

"It has to do with Physics," he said.

"Oh God," I said and rolled my eyes. Here we go again.

"Put in 1.6 x 10 (-33)," he said.

She put the code in, and the screen turned green, and everything popped up.

"How did you know? Hannah asked.

"It's Planck's length," Jackson said.

"Alright, I'm in," Larisa said.

We looked as she worked her magic on her computer screen. She was able to pull up a heat sensor map that showed where people were located. It seemed that there wasn't anybody on the main floor or above. Perfect.

"Alright guys almost done here," she said.

We watched her continue to work on the screens when, finally, we saw the backup lights in the building go off.

"What does that mean?" I asked.

"It means that the security cam system is disabled for 45-minutes while it reboots. You better hurry. Shit, wait a second. Tilt your heads back guys," she said.

We tilted our heads back, and she put drops in our eyes. Suddenly everything became hard to see or keep my eyes open.

"What did you just do to us?" I asked.

"These are the night vision eye drops I was telling you about. Here, put these glasses on until you get inside," she said.

Jackson and I put the glasses on and suddenly we could see clearly, even though it was dark and basically pitch-black.

"Don't forget your shit guys," she said as she handed Jackson the rubber master thumbprint and handed me the Helium tank. She also gave me a duplicate vial of the IC443 vial that I can replace it with. Bitch came prepared.

"Love you guys," I said as I turned and walked with Jackson.

"Wait, one second. I almost forgot," Larisa said as she pulled out three earpieces. We each put one in our ear.

We must have looked like two blind people the way we were wearing the darkest shades at night. Jackson made his way to the front of the building and pressed the master thumbprint up to it. It beeped and turned green and we pushed our way into the building. Once inside we went to the elevator and took it up to the third floor. We got out. Jackson tripped over the helium tank and hit the floor.

"Shhhhhh. Jesus Jackson," I said.

He stood up and brushed himself off. Turned down to the end of the hallway, cupped his hands and screamed.

"DJ KHALED!!!!!!" Jackson said.

"What the fuck are you doing?" I asked.

"Relax Graham, hey Larisa," he said as he put his hand to his head.

"Yeah?"

"Do you see any warm bodies?" He asked.

"Just you two," she said.

"See, relax, nobody is here. We've got this," he said as he removed the vent grate for me. "Now get in the fucking box," he said. I complied.

I took my glasses off and started to inch my way down the heating duct. I was going to have to be quick because in about twenty minutes these things were going to go off. It was freezing in this building. I tunneled my way for what seemed to be an eternity.

"Riss, I'm going to need some guidance here," I said into my earpiece.

"I got you superstar. At the next fork, take a left, then take that down all the way, at the end of that take a quick right, then a quick left and you're right there," she said.

"Copy that," I said as I continued to make my way through. Just as she said, I made a left, then took the long way down, and at the end made a quick right. I came up to another grate. I looked straight up and saw the phone in the bulletproof case, but there was a slit in the back, probably to give the phone some air. PERFECT I thought. I hooked the helium canister up to the tube and snaked it up until I reached the case. After a little finessing, I was able to get it into the case. I turned the Helium on and set my watch for ten minutes. We were going to be cutting this shit extremely close. After the ten minutes was up, I banged on the vent, and Jackson opened the door with the master print. He then came down to the vent and let me out. I pulled the tube out of the box, grabbed the canister and pulled it out, and came out of the tunnel.

I stood up and dusted myself off, it was so dusty in there I had a sneezing fit every two minutes.

"Come on Jax, we don't have much time," I said.

"Roger that. Hey Larisa, how are we doing on time and security?" Jackson asked.

No answer.

"Hello, Larisa. Earth to Larisa," I said.

No answer.

"Shit," Larisa said.

"What?" Jean asked.

"Somebody in the mesh is scrambling all frequency rates from 20-20,000 Hz," she said.

"So, what does that mean?" Hannah asked nervously.

"It means that our boys are on their own for now," she said.

"Come on Jackson, let's get this and get out of here. I don't like this at all," I said.

"Right behind you," he said.

We went to the room where all the vials were being held. It looks like someone cleaned them up since we were last there. We were going to have to find them. I grabbed the thumbprint and put it on the door, and it opened it up. We walked inside and started to open each box delicately to look for the vial. Nothing in the first box, nothing in the second one. This was going to be a problem. Jackson opened up a cabinet to about twenty boxes stacked on each other. We looked at each other, eyes growing wide, cocked our heads to each other and started opening them one at a time. After a few minutes we finally had deliverance.

"Got it!" Jackson said.

I carefully took the vial out and replaced it with the saline one that we were given by Larisa. We closed the door. We left the room just as the Iphone was starting to flicker back on and shut the door.

Our night vision was wearing off a bit, and it was becoming slightly more difficult to see. We took our glasses off to be able to see better, which helped, not going to lie. We walked past the hallway, but must have taken a wrong turn, because we ended up in an unfamiliar place. We used the thumbprint to open the door, and once we walked in, we saw the shock of our life.

"Come on, come on," Larisa said.

"What are you trying to do?" Hannah asked.

"I'm trying to get them back online. Ugh, somebody must have gone in and seen that the security was manually reset instead of its usual cycle," Larisa said.

"Is that going to be a problem?" Hannah asked.

"Only if they're not out in the next fifteen minutes," she said.

We looked around the room. It looked just like a hospital room. There were IV's machines beeping. In the middle of the room was a middle-aged man, with bandages around his neck, unconscious, hooked up to the meter.

"Jesus Christ, what do you think happened here?" Jackson asked.

"Maybe he's patient zero?" I asked.

"We still don't know what this is yet," Jackson reminded me.

"I'm well aware, Jax," I said.

We looked at this person, and I made a split rash decision. I disconnected everything from him that wasn't necessary and started wheeling his bed towards the door.

"What the fuck are you doing?" Jackson asked.

"This person can be the clue to everything," I said. "Come on, help me with this shit," I said.

Jackson and I started rolling the person down the hallway. I picked up my phone and dialed out.

"Who are you calling?" Jackson asked.

"The only people I know of that can help," I said.

I was calling Conrad at Senna Ore. He picked up and we exchanged pleasantries. I explained to him everything that had happened so far. After a joke about how we're keeping his business afloat, I explained to him that we're with a patient, and we need to talk to them, but they're likely in either a medically induced coma or an actual coma. I hung up the phone with him.

"We gotta get out of here. Hey Larisa, are you back online?" I asked.

No answer.

"Shit, alright, let's just go. I remember this hallway, we need to go down and make a right then the elevator should be right there," I said.

We got to the elevator and got in. Just then Larisa came through.

"Guys, are you still there?" She asked.

"Yeah, it's good to hear your voice. Listen we found a . . ." I said as I was cut off.

"No time for that now. Hannah went in after you," she said.

"What?! Why?!" I asked incredulously.

"Because we lost contact with you and you have eight minutes before the system is back online. OH SHIT!" She screamed into our ears.

"Ahhhh, what?" I asked.

"There's another heat body in the building, he's coming right for your elevator," she said.

"Shit," Jackson said as he lifted up the Helium tank with one arm and got ready to launch it at the person. The door slowly creaked open, and we saw Hannah there, with an arm around her neck. It was the janitor.

"Let her go man," Jackson said.

"Oh, I will, don't you worry," he said as he pushed her aside and pulled out his gun and aimed it at the helium tank.

In one fell swoop, Jackson cocked his arm back in rotation and launched the canister at the man, hitting him square in the head, knocking him unconscious. Jackson then went and picked his gun up, unloaded it, took it apart and threw it in the heated vent.

"Baby, are you ok?" Hannah asked me.

"Of course, I am," I said. "Jax, how about you?"

"I'll be fine boss," he said as he rubbed his shoulder. Jackson had surgery on his labrum when he was younger. He was an avid kickboxer, but the bag came at him funny once, and he tore it. Since then, he's worn through all the cartilage that was left in his arm. From time to time it gets sore.

I turned to look to Hannah, and she was smiling at me, but I could tell something was deeply wrong. I hugged her close and felt a rip in the back of her shirt. There was a needle mark in her shoulder and a spec of blood was coming out of it.

"What happened?" I asked, feeling the pit of my stomach again.

"The janitor isn't really the janitor," she began. "I'm infected," she finished.

The world today has 6.8 billion people. That's heading up to about nine billion. Now if we do a really great job on new vaccines, health care & reproductive health services, we could lower that by perhaps 10 or 15 percent. —Bill Gates

Chapter Seventeen

"What the fuck happened in there? And who is that?" Larisa asked.

"We don't know who he is, but we have to get to Senna Ore immediately," I said.

"What why?" She asked.

"I'm infected with the sickness," Hannah said.

"Oh my God. How?" Larisa asked.

"This guy came up to me and told me that I was special, and that I was going to be part of something incredible. Then he covered my mouth and shoved a needle into my back," Hannah said.

"That is the creepiest thing I've ever heard. So, we know for a fact that you're infected," Larisa redirected.

"We don't know shit right now," I began, "all I know is we need to get to Rhode Island as soon as possible," I said.

"Alright, do you have an address?" She asked.

"I know where it is, beautiful. My cousin runs it," Jean said.

I sat in the back seat taking turns between staring at this guy and trying to comfort my wife. This is the worst feeling in the World. It's a helpless trapped feeling. One that alcohol, pills, psilocybin, sleep, everything couldn't take away. The pain was sharp and raw. My heart in my throat pulsating the entire time. My stomach reeling in knots around itself. It took everything in my being to not hurl all over the place. I kept it together best I could for Hannah, but I didn't feel like I was doing a very good job of it.

"Baby, I love you," I said to Hannah.

"I know. You're my mushball, Graham," she replied.

I felt like choking on my tears at that moment but was able to swallow it and keep my composure.

"We're going to figure this out, G," Jackson said. Jackson always called me G when he knew I needed some reassuring comforting words.

We sat and talked for a little bit as Larisa swerved in and out of the surprising traffic that was on the road at this hour of the night. It was hard to stay focused on anything but these two sick people with us.

"Do we even know if this all started at Bionic?" Jean asked.

"We don't know shit right now Jean, I'm hoping that Conrad, Dr. Pivarnick, can help us sort some of this stuff out," I said.

"Well, what about this guy on the bed?" Jean asked.

"I don't know! Look, I panicked, I saw an opportunity and took it. Maybe Senna can, I dunno, wake this guy up. If he's in a medically induced coma, they should be able to reverse the chemicals," I said.

"Won't he wake up on his own since you disconnected everything except his Saline IV?" Jean asked.

That thought hadn't crossed my mind. The idea of this guy waking up and causing a scene in the back of a van, not knowing what he's capable of, suddenly drowned out the remainder of my thoughts.

"I'm just not sure," I said finally. I wasn't mad at Jean, these were legit points. But every time someone looked to me for an answer, all I could do was redirect my thoughts to losing Hannah.

"How are you feeling baby?" I asked her.

"I feel a little woozy," she said.

"Just close your eyes," I said.

I finally convinced her to close her eyes and take a nap. Truth was we were all exhausted. I stayed up and talked with Jackson and Jean for a little while, while Larisa was making good time. Eventually the ancient God Set caught up to me, and I started to doze off.

I was awakened sharply by the sounds of handcuffs hitting the corner of the bed. This guy did wake up, and he was making a scene. We tried to speak to him to calm him down, but it was no use. This guy kept screaming out for someone to put him out of his misery. That's when I saw it.

I turned my eyes to see Hannah. She was looking at me with giant empty eyes. She looked over at the man and at his wrist with the IV sticking in it. She turned to look at me. My life froze for a moment which spanned an eternity. Then in one fluid motion, she took out his IV needle and punctured her Carotid Artery and dragged it across. I screamed and blacked out temporarily. When I came back to, she was bleeding out, and I was trying to keep pressure on her wound, even though I knew deep down it wouldn't work. I was crying and screaming. She reached behind her and opened the back door of the van. Things started flying out the back. Then she undid the hospital bed's safety lock and we watched in horror as the man who was still flailing and screaming rolled out the back of the van and onto oncoming traffic. An 18 wheeler saw him a second too late, turned hard left and side swiped this man. The force knocked the man free of his handcuffs and sent him twenty feet into the air. We were going too fast to see where he landed, but we saw the 18 wheeler start to teeter and then fall over. The sounds of broken glass was haunting for miles. A massive car pileup. By the time I was done looking at this scene, I looked down at Hannah, and she was pale as a ghost, with no life in her eyes. I screamed and punched the van door until my knuckles bled. Then suddenly, as quickly as everything happened, Larisa lost control of the van as we went down the wrong way on the highway, and she broke as hard as she could. We skidded 40 feet and through the marsh on the side and buried the van deep into the swamp. We sat there out of breath, in complete shock, in tears, with vengeance in our hearts. After what seemed like an eternity of this, I heard something.

"Baby."

It was Hannah.

"Baby, wake up," Hannah said.

I opened my eyes, completely covered in sweat and hyperventilating. I've never in my life had such a realistic dream. I sat there looking at Hannah as she was starting to get a little lack of color, smiling at me. I started to brood. I wasn't going to let myself cry in front of her.

"Where are we?" I asked in between yawns.

"We're about 30 miles out. Go back to bed, we'll wake you up," Larisa said.

"Fuck no!" I shouted.

"Alright then," Jackson said.

"You OK Newsdon?" Rosette asked me.

"I'll survive, I think," I said.

Only another 45 minutes until we get to Senna Ore. At the very least we should be able to leave Hannah there while we figure out our next move. They should keep her safe. I asked Jean to turn on the radio. More people in Germany, Ireland, Israel. The death toll worldwide is estimated at half a million people at this point. This is growing exponentially, it's only a matter of time until everybody is caught up with this. We just didn't know that things were about to get much worse for us.

Those who are able to see beyond the shadows and lies of their culture will never be understood, let alone believed, by the masses —Plato

Chapter Eighteen

"Open the door, OPEN THE DOOR!" I screamed into the phone at Conrad. Twenty seconds later both doors swung open, and we wheeled in the unconscious man with Hannah slowly following behind.

"What happened?" Conrad asked.

"She's infected with the sickness," Jean replied.

"I know that cousin, but who the hell is this guy?" Conrad asked.

"We don't know, but we need your help waking him up, I said.

"It just so happens that we have a room for patients here with rare and unexplained syndromes that we treat. I'll have Dr. Pivarnick prepare the room," Conrad said as he walked off. I turned to Hannah.

"Hannah. Whatever this sickness is, whatever it does to your brain to make you go crazy, just know that you'll be safe here. I trust these people with my life," I said.

"I know baby. I'm scared," Hannah said.

I walked over to her and gave her a kiss on her forehead and a big hug. I started to tear up a little but quickly shut it down. There would be none of that. I can't have her seeing weakness in me.

"So first, Hannah, how long ago did you come down with the sickness?" Dr. Pivarnick asked as he and Conrad walked over to us.

"Almost three hours ago," she said.

"Well unfortunately we don't know what this is, so we don't know if there's a latency period. I need you to follow me," Dr. Pivarnick said.

We all walked down the long hallway to the end. There, there was a hospital gown.

"Please my dear. Shower up and change into these," Dr. Pivarnick said.

"OK," she said and disappeared into the shower across the hall. I waited until she shut the door before I addressed them.

"What exactly are you going to do to her?" I asked.

"There's nothing we can do right now, but we're going to lay her on a gurney, strap her down, and monitor her vitals while we figure out what this is. How did she come in contact with this?" Dr. Pivarnick asked.

"She was injected with it. As we were leaving Bionic, a man came around the corner with her in a chokehold, and, when he saw us, he threw her aside and aimed the gun at the helium tank we had. If it wasn't for Jackson's strength, we would all be dead in a terrible explosion," I said as I turned and nodded to Jackson.

"Why did you have a helium tank with you? And why were you at Bionic?" Conrad asked.

"The helium tank is a long story. But we were at Bionic because we were lead there to locate a vial," I said as I removed the vial from my coat pocket and handed it over to Dr. Pivarnick. "We believe that whatever is in here, is the source of the sickness," I said.

"I will get my team to get to work on this right away," Dr. Pivarnick said as he sultered off.

Just then Hannah came out of the room in her hospital gown. Conrad motioned over to another doctor to come over, which he did.

"Are you ready my dear?" Conrad asked.

"I'm scared," Hannah said. I was starting to notice a slight tremor in her hand. I couldn't tell if it was nerves or if it was the sickness.

"My dear, I wish I could say something more comforting to you. We will keep you awake as long as we can monitor until the sickness takes over, so we know the latency time. If it becomes unbearable to you, we can keep you in a medicated coma until we figure this out," Conrad said.

"Will I feel anything?" She asked.

"You won't feel a thing," Conrad said.

"Speaking of coma, can we discuss the other person that we came in with?" Rosette asked.

"Of course. First, my dear after you," Conrad said.

Hannah stepped into the room that was all white which initially gave me a serious sense of anxiety from my bullshit earlier. It was a padded room, one that you would see in a mental institution. There was a bed in the middle of the room with straps to hold someone down. Machines all around to monitor vitals, EEG's etc. The doctor hooked Hannah up to all these machines, then strapped her down.

"I can play some music in this room for you. Also, I can project a movie onto the ceiling if you'd like," the doctor said.

"Music is fine. Thank you," Hannah said.

The doctor came over to her and drew some blood samples. Once he was done, he left the room with them and disappeared down the hall.

"I can promise you that we can keep her safe, that's all I guarantee Graham," Conrad said.

"Thank you," I said. I turned to Conrad and promptly gave him a giant man hug and squeezed him tight.

"You have always been there for us, through the craziest of things. How is it your facility is not expanding?" I asked.

"With national exposure we wouldn't be able to work on the fringe work that we do. We're privately funded as Jean may or may not have explained to you. We work under the radar and put in our two cents through other people if necessary," he finished.

"Um, the other guy?" Rosette asked.

"Right," Conrad said as we walked towards where we left him. He undid the wheel lock and started wheeling this man to another room.

"Graham, you might want to go to the store and get yourself a cup of coffee. We have to hook this man up and do a few tests before we are able to figure out how to proceed," Conrad said.

"Alright," I said.

We all went outside. Caught a breath of sweet fresh air. I lit up a cigarette.

"Those things are going to kill you," Jackson said.

"I have enough things trying to kill me already, Jax," I replied.

We walked two blocks down the road and picked up some sodas and munchies. We then turned and walked back to Senna Ore.

"If they figure out how long it takes people to turn, how does that help us?" Rosette asked.

"If we find the latency period of the sickness, we can backtrack the time it takes for it to show itself, and we can figure out where people were when they caught it," I said.

"I'm glad we're here right now. I actually trust these guys. I've become a little pisanthrophobic in the last few years," Rosette said.

"Yeah me too," I said as I blew out a silver line. I stepped out my cigarette. We had been gone for about twenty minutes. Aside from the moon it was pitch black outside.

"Alright let's head in guys," I said as I motioned for them to follow me.

We went back inside and saw Conrad talking with Dr. Pivarnick. "Ah good, you're back," he said to me.

"What did you find out?" I asked.

"Well it's nothing good. This man has a severe carotid laceration across his throat that looks to be cauterized by what looks like a hot iron. The man is in a coma right now, there's nothing we can do to wake him up," he said.

"FUCK!" I said as I started to feel anxiety. I was picturing Hannah in my dream slicing her throat like this guy must have done.

"There is, however, another option Graham, if you're up to it," Dr. Pivarnick said.

"Yeah, what, anything," I said.

"It's very dangerous though," Conrad said.

"Tell me," I replied.

"Scientists have created something called BrainNet. What they've successfully done was hook three people up to electrodes, and they were able to share thoughts," he began.

"Seriously? I asked incredulously.

"It hasn't gone very far, but it seems promising. Basically, these three people's thoughts were able to play a game similar to Tetris and each of them have a role in it. Direct thought to thought communication hasn't been attempted, but in situations like when you're in a coma, your outside senses are turned off. We monitor the brain waves. The beta waves are hopping around when you're engaged in mental activities. An Alpha wave is prevalent when you're in a state of rest, like when you're walking through the park. The theta waves are when you're in a daydream state. When their consciousness and subconsciousness are flooding you with ideas. Finally, Delta waves would be when you're in a heavy non-REM sleep. Many people coming out of a coma speak about how it felt like a dream or very real like, that they didn't know they were in a coma. The thing is that this person's EEG activity shows a spike in Theta wave. What we're going to have to do is slowly put you under until your brain waves match his and then hopefully, you can enter his 'dream.' This is basically that movie Inception," he said with airquotes.

"This is absolutely bat shit crazy," Rosette said.

"How do you plan on bringing me down to that level," I asked. The thought of having another hallucinatory situation, between the mis-microdosing, the DMT trip, I didn't know if I could handle this alone.

"Jackson, I need you to come with me on this," I turned and faced him.

"You know I'm down for everything. Let's do this," he said.

"Are you sure this is a good idea baby?" Rosette asked.

"How are you bringing us to that level?" I asked.

"We're going to give you propofol and then monitor accordingly," the doctor said.

"Jesus Christ. You mean that shit that killed Michael Jackson?" I asked.

"He was using it day in and day out to go to sleep. That's bananas. We monitor every dose and adjust according to your waves," the doctor said.

"How long do you need to set this up?" I asked.

"About thirty minutes," the Doctor said.

"Fine," I said.

I walked down the hallway to see Hannah again. I opened the door and walked into the room. She was laying there smiling, eyes closed listening to music. I walked up to her and gave her a kiss on the cheek which startled her.

"Hi baby," she said.

"How are you feeling?" I asked.

"Nervous, but other than that, no wish for death," she replied.

"That's good. We're going to figure this out. We're trying something that sounds insane with the patient out there," I said.

"What are you going to do?" She asked.

"We're going to connect to his brain and enter his coma and see if we can get information out of him," I said.

"Oh, that's lovely," she said and giggled and turned around. "You know that sounds insane, right?" She asked.

"You know, everything about Senna Ore since I discovered it has been like a magic show to me. I'm willing to give it a chance. I'd do anything for you," I said.

"I love you. Now go to our friends," she said.

"You mean our family," I replied.

"Exactly," she said.

I gave her another kiss on the cheek and walked out of the room. I went back to everyone as we started discussing the best way to monitor this experiment.

"Wait, Doc, what if I forget that I'm in a coma?" I asked.

"We'll monitor your brain waves, if we see something we don't like, we'll wake you guys up. We'll deal with the fallout later," Conrad replied.

I sat down on the chair outside the room and rubbed my head. This was going to be a long night. Little did I know that Hannah was eventually going to turn, and, unlike previous situations when it was just me or me and Jackson, all our lives were going to be put in danger and we were going to have to make a choice, one that I never thought I would ever get afforded.

Chapter Nineteen

"Alright doc, let's get this started," I said, as I laid down on the gurney.

"Don't sit yet, we have to weigh you. Strip down to your boxers and tee shirt," the doctor said.

I looked over at him confused but did what he said. This must be to measure the anesthesia.

"Alright Graham, you appear to be 200lbs. Jackson, you're about 235," the doctor said.

I know that 200lbs. is not small, but Jackson looks like a linebacker next to me.

"You sure you're ready? We don't even know if this works," Jackson said.

"We need to do this. This guy could be the key to everything," I said.

"You're right. Alright brother, I'm with you," Jackson said as he and I lay down.

They spent a few minutes hooking our brains up to electrodes and setting up our stat machine. Finally, the doctor threaded my vein.

"Alright men, good luck," the doctor said as he turned to Conrad. "Push one milligram per kilogram of weight in 20 mg increments every ten seconds until onset anesthesia. BP 130 over 98 and 100 over 60," the second one was Jacksons. Part of being an athlete. His heart doesn't pump as much. I smoke on the other hand. Conrad did as such and very shortly I felt incredibly dizzy. The next conscious moment I had shocked me.

I was on an Island with blue sand. I looked up to the skies and I saw constellations right at my front door that I've never seen in my life. They looked nothing like the stars that I had become so interested in studying. Out of the corner of my eye I saw Jackson in the water. I walked towards him. The water seemed to repel around him, much like when you stick your hand into a cup of liquid nitrogen, your body heat repels the cold. It's why they tell you never to try it with gloves on because the nitrogen can stick to it and burn you. Interesting phenomenon. At this moment I'm watching Jackson just enjoying his time in the water. I tried to speak out, but no sound came out. I turned to Jackson and thought what I wanted to say. I was about to try and respond when I got a response.

"What is this place?" Jackson's voice asked me in my head.

"I have no idea," I replied. I was yet in another situation where telepathy was the prevalent means of communication.

"You're in the Jellyfish Nebula," another voice said to me and startled me. I turned around and saw the man we came to speak with.

"Where exactly are we?" I asked.

"This is a mental manifestation of my deepest inner thoughts. This physical place is not real, but God dammit isn't it beautiful?" He asked.

"But the stars?" I asked.

"Right there, you recognize those don't you?" He asked.

I looked up for a moment and then it clicked.

"Castor and Pollux," I said. After I said that, I immediately thought of a Hollywood blockbuster I had previously seen that my brother loved called Face Off. The two evil brothers in the movie were Castor and Pollux Troy. The good guy in the movie was Sean Archer. Archer like Sagittarius with the bow and arrow. Gemini and Sagittarius as opposing signs. I don't think I could turn my mind off regarding this if I tried.

"What is your name?" Jackson asked.

"My name is Franco," he replied.

"Well Franco, I don't know if you know this, but back on Earth we're having a bit of a problem. People are coming down with a sickness that causes them to take their life," I said.

"I know," I heard him say, "I've never felt pain and fear like that before."

"You do know you're in a coma?" Jackson asked him.

"All I know is that I'm at complete peace here. There's no negativity, no violence, no anger, no fear, no pain. I'm in the most beautiful environment I've ever been in," Franco said.

"How did we get here so fast?" I asked.

"It was instantaneous Graham. Our souls must have quantum tunneled," Jackson said.

I didn't want to get involved with that right now. I turned to Franco and he nodded.

"I know that I can go back if I want to, I've made it clear that it's not my time. But what's the point. I'm in Heaven right now," Franco said.

"Look, we're not here to convince you to come back. We are going to find a cure though," I said.

"And then what? Go through all that physical and mental pain again. Go through physical therapy, psych watch? I'm depressed. I was on 6 pills a day just to balance my mind. I don't have to worry about any of that here. Did I mention also that there's no fear here?" Franco continued.

"What happened to you?" I asked.

Franco bent over and picked up a handful of sand and let it slip through his fingers slowly, each piece sparkling like a diamond in the sky. "I was the first," he finally said.

"The first at what?" Jackson asked.

"In Europe scientists had figured out a way to remove the protein out of a certain jellyfish that glowed and were going to use it to make trees that light up. They would plant it, and then in a hundred years, there would be no need for streetlights. That had a lot of people worried because, if they can't make money off it, what good would it do. It was through the constant look at the jellyfish that another anomaly was discovered. There is also a certain type of jellyfish that when it stings you, shortly thereafter you get an immediate impending sense of doom. The problem is that it is only localized in one area of the world. Secondary to that, you couldn't exactly go around stinging people with a jellyfish. The military figured this out and wanted to find a way to weaponize that protein. They offered the top research scientists in the US almost unlimited funds to further their other projects if they would prioritize this one. A top secret meeting was held and the military decided that this was the wave of the future. It would save drastic amounts of money on weaponry. If you could just find a way to infect the enemy with it, they would kill themselves. They began working on this, testing it and they found that there was one way that it would work flawlessly. They modified the protein and put it in injections. But it had to go with something else. The people that were pulling the strings on the higher ups started chiming in. They thought this was a wonderful way to depopulate the planet. But how would they be able to do that? Who voluntarily gets shots?" Franco asked.

"Vaccines," I said as I could feel myself slowly being pulled away from this entire setting. Like I was being sucked back.

"I don't like his wave pattern right there. Push another 10mg, we might have underestimated his tolerance," the doctor said.

All at once I felt like I was back with Franco and Jackson.

"Exactly. Now this is where I came in. I was the head of R&D at Bionic. I had a conference call with some very scary people, people that work behind the scenes, the kind of people who decide who gets to live or die and assured me that this would only be used for military purposes. They also offered R&D at Bionic double our companies net worth to perfect the formula. See when you get stung with the jellyfish, within half an hour you would start to see symptoms," Franco continued.

"So, what did you do?" I asked.

"Well it does nobody any good if they go in for a vaccine and then thirty minutes later they kill themselves. That would be too easy to trace. Our job in R&D was to figure out a way to delay the onset of symptoms by about two days and that's exactly what we did," Franco said.

"What happened to you?" I asked.

"I was accidentally cc'd on an email thread from one of these powerful people explaining that they had given Bionic money as well as other major pharma/vaccine producers in Boston, Raleigh-Durham, San Diego. He said something about Saturn losing its rings or something and explained that this would be used for depopulation in the World," Franco said.

I bit my tongue on the Saturn part. "How did you get infected with the sickness?" I asked.

"I started watching TV late at night because I couldn't sleep. They kept talking about the universal flu vaccine that they were rolling out. The one that Bill Gates convinced our President that would be incredibly beneficial. Everything just clicked with me. They were going to compromise the universal flu vaccine that was being rolled out all over the world. Once I figured that out, I reached out in an email to my higher ups. About thirty minutes later I received a text message to meet at Bionic with all the information I had. I went there and I had a bag over my head and was brought into a room. The next thing I knew, the bag came off and I saw some very menacing people that said they had plans for me. That I was doing a great service for my country. I was injected with the first solution. They kept me in that room for two days as it was the weekend, and nobody was coming into the building. At the 50th hour, and I know this because they kept a running clock, I started feeling this incredible emptiness inside me. Worthlessness. Then it became something altogether different. Something I never thought I'd feel," Franco said.

"What was that?" I asked.

"The will to live left my body entirely, and I wanted to kill myself. I BEGGED the men to do it for me. Instead, they left a piece of glass in my reach. I grabbed it and sliced my neck. I blacked out. You're the first people I've come in contact with since that happened," Franco said.

"Jesus," I said.

"No kidding," Franco said. "But they did forget one very important thing," he said.

"What's that?" I asked.

"I printed out everything I had on this and locked it in my safe at home. Combination is 122112. End of the world, right?" He laughed.

"Where do you live?" I asked.

"In Duxbury. Crystal Lane. 453. Key is under the mat," he said.

"Are you sure you don't want to come back with us? How do we even go back?" I asked.

"It's pretty simple, and no. Come back and get me when you find a cure for this thing. All I know is that each disease has a weakness, you just have to read the signs," he said.

"And how do we get out of here?" Jackson asked.

"Wait for a shooting star and generate your entire energy towards it," he said as he smiled and walked off into the distance and disappeared.

We waited for what seemed like an eternity. Finally, one started to pass, and we did just that.

"Their Theta waves have plateau'd and haven't changed in a few minutes. We need to wake them up," the doctor said as he pushed the reversing agent into our bodies. And just like that, we were back in the room in Senna Ore.

"What did you guys see? Did you meet him?" Rosette asked.

"We need to get over to Duxbury right now," I said.

"So, you did see something," she said.

"I'll explain along the way," I said as I looked at my watch. We had a day and a half left before Hannah would be joining Mr. Franco.

"Can somebody explain to me what's going on here?" Jean asked.

"Everything we need is at that man's house in his safe," I said as I pointed to Franco.

"Wait, you mean you really had a conversation with him?" Larisa asked.

"I'll explain along the way. Jean, you're driving. Me and Jax can't, we just came out of anesthesia," I said.

"Well what about me?" Larisa asked.

"I need you for something else," I said.

We said our goodbyes to Conrad and the Doctor, and I walked over to Hannah's room. She was asleep at this point, and I didn't want to wake her. Didn't know what kind of condition she would be in if I did. I did have a suspicious feeling that just because it took Franco 50 hours, doesn't mean it's the same for all people. It's probably much less for her since she's so tiny.

We piled into the car and Jean stepped on the gas. The one thing I didn't expect was the Devil talking to Jesus on the mountain in my near future.

There are three classes of people. Those who see. Those who see when they are shown. Those who do not see —Leonardo Da Vinci

Chapter Twenty

"Everybody back in the van," I said as I slowly walked towards the door. The propofol was still in my system, and I felt like I had been ripped out of deep DMT flowing REM sleep into reality. I was assured by Dr. Pivarnick that would go away shortly. We got in the van and started making our way to Duxbury.

"Hey Riss," I started.

"Yeah hun," she said.

"I need you to scope out his home and see if he has a security system monitoring it," I said.

"On it," she said.

We had a few hour's drive to where we had to go. Jackson and I filled everyone in on Franco and what we learned. Jean raised concerns that there was a possibility that it wasn't real, to which I countered that Jackson has the same memory of what happened as I did, so there was a good chance it wasn't that.

"Ok guys, so here's the thing," Larisa began, "he has a complicated tier security system. It's going to take me a little while to get in. It's being monitored by a network 24/7. Anytime a body comes to the sensor, it starts recording in live time. If it's a person that's not supposed to be there, they will alert the police and be there shortly. The police station is not far from his house," Larisa said.

"So, what can you do about it?" Jean asked.

"I'm going to worm in and create a 30 second loop that continuously plays. When they look at the monitors, they will see nothing, so nothing will be alerted," she said as she ruffled her hair and pulled down her face. You could tell that she was getting tired and that all this hacking was getting to her.

"Let me know once that's done," I said.

"Roger that captain," she said.

We continued to talk about our next steps while I shook off this coma. Jackson was in the corner in and out of consciousness. Propofol is based on body weight, and he had a lot more in his system than I did. I began to wonder if they overmedicated him.

"Mon ami," Jean began, "What is the next plan assuming we get in the house and find what we're looking for?" He asked.

"I haven't really gotten that far Jean," I began, "I think if we can get the plans for the sickness, we should be able to have Larisa release it online and in the dark web, maybe to Anonymous and let it take its course," I said.

"What about the President?" Rosette asked.

"That's a good point. OK, so assuming all goes well, I will reach out to the old email that Lilac Northinly had. See if it's archived or live still. I could also reach out to Blur and have him get that out. The only thing I'm worried about is in the wrong hands, they might be able to weaponize this further. If anybody finds out that Senna Ore has a vial of this, the facility and everybody inside would be burned to the ground, including Hannah and Franco. I'm not willing to risk that yet. Let's just see what happens once we get to the house," I said.

We sat and talked for a few more hours until we got to Duxbury. At this point I woke Jackson, and we all put on our heightened senses.

"Riss, are we good?" I asked.

"Yeah, just finished. I figure we have about twenty minutes before anybody runs a routine scan and notices something wrong, so let's be in and out," she said.

"In and out. I like it," Jean said and smiled to his girlfriend. Larisa rolled her eyes.

"Alright enough of that. Let's do this thing," I said.

We pulled up to the block and parked two houses down. It was about ten o' clock at night, and everybody was in their house, sleeping. I walked up to the front door and lifted the mat as Franco advised. There was a key under it. I picked it up, unlocked the door and we stepped inside.

The house was shockingly unremarkable. It was completely void of personal effects. From the outside there was a garden, and the grass was cut, but inside, not so much was taken care of. We immediately split up and started looking for this safe he was talking about. Larisa quickly found the computer but noticed that the hard drive was removed. Did someone get here first? Larisa kept looking for a laptop or something of use. I went downstairs and looked around. There was nothing downstairs but a tv in the corner and a leather recliner. Honestly, either this guy is the worst bachelor ever, or this is a temporary house. I opened one sliding door, and it was the washer and dryer. Closed the door. I turned around and noticed a pocket door a quarter of the way open. I opened it all the way and found the safe. I quickly alerted everyone, and then opened it with the code that Franco had given us. The safe beeped, then a green light came on, and it opened. Inside was a stash of money, some passports, a hard drive and an envelope full of documents.

"Hey Riss, come down here a minute," I said.

Larisa made her way downstairs, and I handed her the hard drive. She smiled and went back upstairs to the computer in the living room. I opened the manila envelope. It was everything that I thought it was going to be.

There were orders from a secret sect describing what the mission was. To reduce the population by 100 million people in the first two years. There was all sorts of scientific data that I didn't understand, but basically from what I could gather was that they were going to go country by country and introduce what they called 'the solution' which we call 'the sickness' slowly. Then faster and faster to make people think that it's a virus. There were plans in here to stage a false flag operation on the WHO organization to dump the whole World into chaos. I just shook my head and made my way upstairs.

"Hey Graham," Larisa yelled from upstairs.

"Yeah?" I replied.

"Got a problem here. Need your help," she said.

"What is it?" I asked from downstairs.

"There's a password on this, and it will wipe the computer clean if it's not entered correctly," she said.

Not this shit again. I thought to myself.

"What does it say?" I asked.

"Can you just come up here. Too much to yell," she said.

I walked up the stairs and walked over to the computer. Larisa had installed the hard drive, but there was a password block on it.

"And there arose much godlessness, and they committed fornication, and they were led astray, and became corrupt in all their ways. Semjaza taught enchantments, and root-cuttings. Armaros the resolving of enchantments, Baraqijal taught astrology, Kokabel the constellations, Ezeqeel the knowledge of the clouds, Araqiel the signs of the earth, Shamsiel the signs of the sun, and Sariel the course of the moon. Password is five digits," she said.

"He did not die, he walked faithfully with God," I said.

"What?" She asked.

"It's Enoch," I said.

She punched Enoch into the computer, and it opened up like a lotus flower.

"I don't understand. The book of Enoch isn't even in the Bible. Is every ancient story about astrology and astronomy?" She asked.

"It would appear that way. The only thing I haven't been able to figure out is WHY the four gospels were selected over the others. Did you know that Satan had a Gospel?" I asked everyone.

"Did not know that. Hey, can we hurry this up, I've got a bad feeling about being here," Jackson said.

"I think I have it," Larisa said.

"What are you doing girl?" I asked.

"I'm making a backup of all the files on this computer. I think he digitized that envelope you have in your hands," Larisa said.

"How much time do you need to back it up to your flash drive?" I asked.

"About ten minutes," she said.

Just as I was about to say OK, we heard a window shatter. Someone had thrown a Molotov Cocktail through the big front window and half the living room was on fire. It was blocking the front door out.

The more powerful and original a mind, the more it will incline towards the religion of solitude

—Aldous Huxley

Chapter Twenty-One

"Holy shit!" Jean screamed.

Jackson looked around him and ran into the kitchen. He ran back out with a fire extinguisher that was attached to the wall. He pulled the pin and tried to spray the fire, it only contained it, but there wasn't enough to put it out, and it was still blocking our only way out. We couldn't jump out the window because the fire was there too.

"Somebody do something, I can't lose these files," Larisa said.

The fire was roaring, the flames dancing in the moonlight. We started to cough a little from the CO_2 being let off.

"Larisa, we have to go!" I screamed.

"Just a few more minutes," she said.

"We don't have time, mon Cherie," Jean said.

Then out of the corner of my eye I saw Rosette's eyes light up. She went over to the flower vases that were on the dining room table, she looked it over. There was an image of Aquarius pouring his ambrosia over a fire. She picked up the two vases and threw them at the two places where the fire was most prevalent. After about eight seconds, the fire completely subsided. It was as if it was swallowed into a black hole of itself. She looked over at me and half smiled and shrugged her shoulders.

"What in the hell was that?" I asked.

"At first, I was looking for more water to throw, but then I noticed the symbol on the side. This isn't a normal house. How there's nothing in it of personal value. Everything here is functional," she began, "The vases are called firevases and they're made by Samsung. They were enclosed around Potassium Carbonate. It's a pretty new fire extinguishing method. It's a vase, you can put flowers in it, but in case of a fire, you launch this to the fire, it shatters and releases the compound. It basically sucks out all the oxygen in the room. What does a fire need to survive?" She asked.

"Oxygen," Jackson said.

"Exactly. This isn't a personal home, this is a safe house," Rosette said. "Someone outside knows we're here, clearly," Rosette said.

"You done Riss?" I asked.

"Done. Let's get the fuck out of here," she said.

We collected our things and opened the door and stepped outside. Once we did, we were met by three men with guns drawn on us.

"Let's go for a little drive," the first man said. "But first," he began as he raised his gun to my head, "the envelope and the hard drive please," the man said.

I walked over towards him defeated. This was all the proof in the world regarding the sickness, and once gone, we had nothing. I handed the man the envelope and the hard drive.

"And the flash drive in your purse miss," the man said.

"What?" Larisa asked.

"Please don't make me ask you again," he said as he cocked his gun and lifted it in the air twice to indicate her to hurry up.

Larisa sludged over to this man and handed him the flash drive.

"How did you know I had a flash drive?" Larisa asked.

"We've been watching you since we wormed into the home monitoring system. You're good, but you left a backdoor to your loop. Not your fault, you were in a rush. Now, as I was saying, I'm riding with you, get in the van," the first man said as he launched another Molotov Cocktail into the house. Immediately it burst into flames and spread like wildfire, literally. By the time we turned the corner, the entire house was already up in flames.

Once men died for Truth, but now truth dies at the hands of men —Manly P Hall

Chapter Twenty-Two

"Where are we going?" I asked this man.

"You'll know soon enough," the man replied.

"Who are you?" Rosette asked.

"You can call me Dr. Spear," the man said.

"Spear, as in the house of Spear?" I asked.

The man grinned widely, and then his smile just as quickly disappeared.

It had occurred to me once again about Cain and Abel. Cain the Spear, and the Spear in the side of Jesus. Was this man's bloodline a part of that?

"Take a left here and get on the highway," Dr. Spear said.

"Jackson, just do what he says," Jean said.

"I am, relax," Jackson said. He was trying to be cool and collective, but you could see the veins in his arms and biceps pounding. He seemed to be more angry than scared to have a gun in his face. It's happened to me so many times at this point, I was kind of numb to it.

"You guys are, and I don't say this lightly, literally the biggest pain in the ass that we've dealt with. Every time we think we have something figured out, your name pops up Mr. Newsdon. To be honest, I'm kind of impressed that you have made it this far in life without having been killed," Dr. Spear said.

"I was shot in Israel," I said.

"Israel, Israel," Dr. Spear said as if he was searching for something. "Oh yes, your little squabble with those two societies. That's chicken shit stuff honestly. I have been following your work on Aquastream though, and I must say, you've figured out a lot of things haven't you. People have literally been dismembered for knowing 1/100th of what you know. Why do you think it is that you're alive right now?" Dr. Spear asked.

"I've been asking myself that for a while now. My book, my video channel, my legacy. Not that many people get to find a calling in life. I just want to make my mark," I said.

"I appreciate your honesty, it's a refreshing characteristic for people your age. But again I ask, why are you still alive?" Dr. Spear asked. "I could very easily waste all of you here right now. Get off on the next exit," he said.

"Pure luck," I said.

"You're alive because we've kept you alive. See, at first we didn't know what to make of you, your brother and the President. But we had no idea that us having the

President sign the orders on your brother's demise would impact you so much. You were not even on the radar for months. Then you discovered the capstones. That threw us off guard. There's no way that we would have been able to figure out all that you've figured out to get them. So, we started paying attention. When the Rosicrucians and the Knights Templar started having a fight in our own backyard, your name once again popped up. This time we listened. Your book came out and hit the best sellers list. People wondering when you'll release another one. For 8,000 years, everything has been ruled by as above, so below. You were able to trace from the Egyptians, to the Jews, to the Christians, and the next step would be the new Age of Aquarius. There were talks to have you all wiped out, but two things. It would have only caused the Streisand effect and boosted your sales and rumors of your demise, but two, we are able with all the information you've leaked to change the narrative," Dr. Spear said.

"And that's why you released the sickness on everyone," I said.

"Once this sickness gets going, people will be praying to God and to anyone who can help them. We will provide them with a cure, after a few years of this. The population will be so grateful, we will be able to implement new laws across the countries that they can follow.

See, the Age of Aquarius is about a New World Order, but not the type of bullshit that President George HW Bush talked about on live TV. But a true one world government, one world religion," Dr. Spear said.

"Why are you keeping us alive right now?" I asked.

"We're getting off right here. Park the car right by that speedboat," Dr. Spear said.

We got out of the car and started walking towards the speedboat. The two men exited their Escalade and followed behind us, guns trained on us.

"I'm sorry for all of this Graham," the older man said.

I recognized that voice. "Dr. Rorja. Is that you?" I asked.

"I'm sorry Graham," Dr. Rorja said.

"How could you, after everything that you've helped us out with?" I asked.

"This wasn't the easiest decision I've ever had to make Graham, but I have to think about my only son, Logan," he said as he motioned over to the man standing next to him. Upon closer inspection, I saw a young teenager holding a gun trembling.

"You don't have to do this kid, you know that right?" I asked him.

"Don't speak to him," Dr. Rorja said as he cocked his gun and aimed it at me.

Just then I got a phone call. Everybody looked at me like I just got them killed.

"Well go ahead and answer it," Dr. Spear said as he motioned to me with the gun to pick it up.

"Hello?" I asked.

"Graham, I've been trying to reach you, is everything ok?" Conrad asked.

I was silent.

"Sniff if you're in trouble right now," he said to me.

I sniffled.

"I'm sending police to your coordinates right now. I just wanted to tell you that Hannah has turned, but we've been managing to keep her relatively sedated. We're working up a few ideas. I'll get back to you shortly," Conrad said as he hung up.

"Who was that?" Dr. Rorja asked.

"That was the man who's with Hannah right now. She's been infected with the sickness," I said.

"That's a shame Graham. There will be a cure one day. I hope you will be around to see it," Dr. Spear said.

"What are we doing at this beach right now?" Rosette asked.

"First, everyone take out their phones and hand them to me," Dr. Spear said.

One by one, we took our phones out and handed them to him. He put them in a metal garbage can that was a few feet away. Then he took out the flash drive, the hard drive and the envelope and put it in there, too. Then he calmly went back to his Escalade and came back with a Molotov Cocktail. He lit the rag at the end of it and threw it into the garbage can. Everything exploded into a giant ball of flame and settled on a roasting fire. Just then the police came by. My heart jumped to my throat.

"Good evening officer," Dr. Spear said.

"What's going on here this evening? We got a call that there was a disturbance," the first officer said.

"Nothing really, just a little bonfire to start the night off," Dr. Spear said.

Just then the lithium batteries in our phones exploded and rocked everyone back a few feet.

The first police officer looked over to our faces and saw that something was wrong.

"Sir, you're going to need to step over here with me," the first officer said.

"That won't be necessary," Dr. Spear said as he pulled out an all white ID card and then pointed to the all white license plates.

"Oh, I'm sorry sir. I didn't realize. Well, carry on," the first police officer said.

"What's going on?" The second police officer asked.

"Nothing, I'll explain to you in the car," the first officer said as they turned to leave and got in their squad car and left. My heart that was in my throat, dropped down into my ass.

"You see that Graham. That's power that money cannot buy," Dr. Spear said. "Now everyone, get in the speedboat," he finished.

We got into the speedboat for the short ride. Duxbury beach has a beach within a beach. After a two-minute ride, we were on a beach that was a couple hundred meters into the water. We all stepped off.

"I want the women to the left, and the men to the right," Dr. Spear said.

We separated as asked.

"Graham, you saw what happened there with the police? We are protected. We own them. We own the police, the judges, the politicians, the banks, wherever you think the power lies, we have it. I want to extend that to you," Dr. Spear said.

"Excuse me?" I asked bewildered.

"There's that old adage that says if you can't beat 'em join 'em. Graham, think about it. I'm offering you the keys to the world. You already know how everything is run, so that's easy. You can have all the money in the world. You can keep writing best sellers, you can have millions more on your Aquastream account. You can fight the greatest fights in the world. You'll never have to worry about a thing. All we ask is that you let this 'sickness,' as you call it, play out the way it's supposed to. Hell, we can even have you help out writing the new religion of the new age. What do you say?" Dr. Spear asked.

"You came all this way just to ask me to stand down?" I asked, even more bewildered.

"And to offer you paradise on earth. Anything you ever want. You want to take down the Catholic Church for good, we can help with that. They're old news anyway, it's about time they met their end. You want to know the great secrets of the world? We have volumes of books that will make your head spin. If you think you know anything right now, believe me, you don't know shit. Do you even know what's going on in Antarctica right now?" He asked.

I shook my head no.

"Exactly. I'm aware that you're going to have to make a quick decision on this, but I will allow your friends here to come along for the ride. I can promise you immunity from the sickness. I can protect you all. All I require is your allegiance. Just think about it," Dr. Spear said as he turned to talk to Dr. Rorja and his son.

I turned back to my friends. I'm not going to lie, I know what the noble thing is to do right now, but a part of me really wonders if I could gain access to all this sacred information, what good it could do if I released it all. I'm guessing that not many people are offered what I was offered just now. Everybody was staring at me and shaking their head no. I turned back just in time to catch Dr. Spear turning to me.

"If I climb on board with this, what do you need from me?" I asked.

"Are you negotiating?" Dr. Spear asked.

"I am," I said to the horror and dismay of my friends. "I'm sorry but the allure of all this secret information that I could release and make the smaller newer population more intelligent, even raise their vibration another level, is too intoxicating," I said.

"This requires a sacrifice, you know Graham?" Dr. Spear said.

"What kind of sacrifice? Like an animal?" I asked.

"No, human," Dr. Spear asked as he tossed his gun to me. "Have you ever heard of the trolley problem?" He asked.

I had but I shook my head no so that I could hopefully buy us some more time to figure out how to get the fuck out of here.

"There's a rail switch and a train coming. On one side are two people tied to the tracks (as he nodded over to Jackson and Jean), and on the other side there's two people tied to the tracks (as he turned and nodded over to Rosette and Larisa). You have to flip the switch, one of them has to go. Who's it going to be?" He asked.

"Are you telling me that I have to kill either the men in my life, or the women?" I asked.

"If you're serious about this commitment. Everybody that's ever been a member this high up has made this decision," Dr. Spear said.

"I don't know if I can do this," I said.

"Sure, you can. Just pick one, do it quick than deal with the fallout later. The other two will forgive you eventually. Or would you rather die here, all five of you?" Dr. Spear asked.

I sat and turned to them. Everything that we've been through was flashing through my eyes. This is the first time I've been in this situation.

"And don't think of shooting me either," Dr. Spear said as Dr. Rorja and Logan aimed their guns at me.

I chambered a round and opened the clip. There were still a few bullets left in there. I turned to Dr. Spear and held the gun up to my head.

"Interesting Zodiac boy. Where are you going with this?" Dr. Spear asked.

"Murder is not something I'm willing to live with," I said.

"Oh really? So, what do you call Marshall in Israel with the pyramid?" Dr. Spear asked.

I was bewildered at how he knew about that. I thought we got out of there scott free.

"You do realize that I have the ability to destroy you with all the information that you haven't shared with the public, right?" Dr. Spear said.

I slowly pulled the gun down. I had come to the realization that if I shot myself, they would just kill the rest of them. If I shot Dr. Spear, than Dr. Rorja would have shot all of us. But if I shot two of my friends, that would be the end of it. This is the ultimate trolley problem. I slowly raised my arm up and aimed at Jean's head.

Right up until this exact moment, a very small part of me still had resentment towards Jean for NP's death. Until this moment. Until I was put in literally the same situation that he was in. I knew everything that went through his head, all the raw emotions, all the fear. It was overpowering. At the end, like him, I had to make a choice. "Je suis desole, mon amis," I said as I put my finger around the trigger. Suddenly I heard a loud noise and a scream. I turned and saw that Logan was holding a bloodied brick over his head and Dr. Spear was on the floor.

"What are you doing?" Dr. Spear asked.

"This is for my brothers," Logan said as he slammed the brick on his head again. Dr. Spear's head hit the sand and his glasses flew off.

"You're a dead man. You're both dead men walking," Dr. Spear said.

"We've already been dead," Dr. Rorja said as he fired a round into Dr. Spear's head.

I think 99 times and find nothing. I stop thinking, swim in the silence and the truth comes to me

—*Albert Einstein*

Chapter Twenty-Three

We sat there stunned as the events unfolded in front of us. I was completely certain I was going to have to kill my friends in order to let the girls live. I was hoping this wasn't going to be a problem in the future for us.

"What the hell was that all about?" Rosette asked.

"I'm sorry you guys, but me coming here was the only way that I would be sure that you guys would survive. I brought my son with me because I couldn't trust that he wouldn't be killed if he stayed back in Switzerland. The truth of the matter is that this is a long time coming," Dr. Rorja said.

"What was a long time coming?" Jean asked.

"This consulate has become more erratic as the years went by. First it was to control the natural resources, then eventually it became to control the population of the World. I can't in good conscience stand by while Millions if not Billions of people are slaughtered. Unfortunately, all the proof has been destroyed in that fire," he said.

"I wouldn't be so sure of that," Larisa said.

Dr. Rorja's eyes spread wide. "What do you mean darling?" He asked.

"I backed everything up to my phone. Granted, the phone was destroyed in the fire, but he never made me take this bracelet off," she said.

We sat there and looked at her as she turned her orange bracelet on. A light from the middle of it projected her phone onto her wrist.

"This is called the cicret bracelet. This is a functioning phone on my wrist. I have all the files right here," she said to everyone's bewilderment.

"That is a clever girl," Dr. Rorja began, "I'm well aware that if all this goes as planned that I could be going away for a long time, if not be killed. All of us at the Consulate. But if I am to meet my maker, after all I've done in my life, I can go there with a clear conscience," he concluded as he picked up the body of Dr. Spear and dropped him in the speedboat. "You guys need to get the hell out of here. You'll probably never see me again, but it was great to finally meet the great Graham Newsdon and his friends," Dr. Rorja said as he motioned to his son to get in the boat. They both got in the speedboat as did we, and they dropped us off back at shore. Then, Dr. Rorja handed us the keys to the Escalade and gave Jackson his gun.

"This vehicle will protect you. We'll dispose of this body shortly," he said ominously and then he and his son sped off.

We checked the garbage can to see if anything could be salvaged, but everything was just charred and melted together. We got in the Escalade, we figured the van was spotted now and we were going to call it stolen when we got back to Quincy. We got into the Escalade and started the car. As soon as the ignition kicked in, we saw the front window spider crack as somebody was shooting at us.

Religion is one of the safest places to hide from God
—Richard Rohr

Chapter Twenty-Four

It was one man in an unmarked car that was shooting our car up. Thankfully, the entire car was bullet proof glass. You could hear the man cursing outside of the vehicle as he unloaded another clip into the front windshield. We wondered how long it was going to hold up. Jackson chambered a round and looked as if he was going to jump out, until Rosette grabbed his arm and shook her head violently no.

"Come out of the vehicle please," the man asked.

We sat there silent, there was no way we were getting out of the vehicle. Unfortunately, the entire front windshield was completely cracked at this point and nearly impossible to see out of.

"I shall ask you one more time. Where is Dr. Spear? I'm going to count to ten, and then I'm going to come physically drag you out. If I have to do that, it's not going to be pretty for you," the man said.

We sat there as he counted from 1-10 slowly. All Jackson could do was hold the gun to the window.

"Hey guys, cover your ears," Jackson said.

We all did.

"I thought we could do this diplomatically, but I guess you guys aren't in the business of that. Never mind then," the man said as he slowly walked towards the driver's side and loaded another clip into his gun.

"This is it guys," Jackson said as he held the gun up to the window. Before the man could open the car door, Jackson must have gotten nervous and fired a round at the window. To everyone's surprise the bullet went through the window and hit the man in the stomach. He flung his gun to the sand a few feet away and hit the ground.

"How is this possible? Larisa asked.

"I'd heard rumors that you could manufacture one-way bullet proof glass, I'd just never seen it from my own eyes before," I said.

Jackson got out of the car, gun trained on this man on the floor. We all got out as well.

"Who are you?" Jackson asked.

"I'm the backup. Dr. Spear activated his distress signal and I came. Where is he?" The man said as he winced through pain.

"He's dead," I said.

"What?" He asked incredulously.

"It wasn't us," Jackson said as he trained the gun on this man.

"Doesn't matter, you're all too late. This solution has spread too far too quick. There's no way to go back," the man said and laughed, and he coughed and spit up a wad of blood onto the sand.

"Come on Jackson let's go," Larisa said.

"No, I'm not leaving him like this," Jackson said.

"What are you going to do? Shoot me again?" The man asked.

Without hesitation, Jackson took the gun and shot the man through the heart. He laid there dead.

"Oh my God baby, what did you just do?" Rosette asked.

"The stakes are too high right now. We've got to figure out what we're going to do with the information we have," Jackson said.

"Well the first thing we'll have to do is send it to Senna Ore and Conrad. Maybe it will help them," I said.

"On it," Larisa said as she activated her hologram watch again and sent an email over to Conrad.

"The only problem with this watch is there's no speaker. We can't answer the phone calls that come in," she said.

"Alright, so we have to go get phones then," I said.

"They're probably tracking our cell phones already. We don't know what the Consulate is capable of," Jackson said.

"Good point, everyone in the van. We'll go pick up a few burners," I said.

We left this man on the beach, Jackson cocked back and launched the gun into the water. We got in the van and then started our drive to the nearest 24/7 convenience store to pick up a few cell phones. What was the next step?

The object of life is not to be on the side of the majority, but to escape finding oneself in the ranks of the insane —Marcus Aurelius

Chapter Twenty-Five

2 days later

"What exactly happened in Duxbury?" Dr. Dotpun asked Dr. Rorja.

Dr. Rorja stayed silent for a minute, puffing on his pipe that he seldom used unless he was wracked with nerves. "Everything went wrong," he finally said.

"Care to elaborate on that?" Dr. Magnor asked.

"What exactly happened to Dr. Spear? Did you give those kids the 'Devils promise' as discussed?" Dr. Schrodhilt asked.

"We did," Dr. Rorja spoke as his son sat quietly in the corner.

"Well, what happened. Did Graham choose?" Dr. Taros asked.

"He did make a choice," Dr. Rorja said. Technically he wasn't lying, Graham was about to shoot the men and leave the women.

"What happened to Dr. Spear, again I ask," Dr. Schrodhilt asked.

"He hit his head and fell off the boat. We tried to grab him, but there was a riptide, and it pulled him out to the water and under it. There was nothing we could do to help him," Dr. Rorja said.

"Was he drunk?" Dr. Magnor asked, becoming very uneasy knowing their 'speaker' was gone now.

"Hard to tell honestly. He hadn't been acting in his right mind from the moment we got there," Dr. Rorja said.

"So, what now?" Dr. Magnor asked.

"I'm sure we'll find out sooner or later," Dr. Rorja said. It was just then that he received a text from an untraceable number telling him that The Marines, SAS, and Israeli Special Forces were on their way to them. They had been found in egregious behavior and were going to be charged with conspiracy to commit terrorism and terrorism. They would cut a deal for him for allowing them to survive, but it would be his job to keep them in Switzerland for another couple of hours. The text signed off Riss. He knew that must have been Larisa. He had wondered how he got her email address or, more importantly, how she was able to salvage the information that was burned down in the garbage can.

"I say we get the fuck out of here. Go back to our respective cities. People will surely put two and two together eventually," Dr. Schrodhilt said.

"No, it's best we stay here. We're in a forcefield here. It's impenetrable," Dr. Rorja said.

"Why are we so sure that somebody is coming for us?" Dr. Magnor asked.

"Let's just come up with an exit strategy," Dr. Rorja started. "How much are you liquid right now?" He asked them.

"About 450 million," Dr. Schrodhilt said.

"If I exercise the Queen's favor, probably about a billion dollars," Dr. Magnor said.

"Alright. So let's fire up the jet for tonight and head to Russia. They can't extradite from there," Dr. Rorja suggested.

"Good idea," Dr. Magnor replied.

The men left the room to their respective cabin and began packing. He could hear them in the background calling in different offshore accounts, and personal helpers to bring them a supply of money. The tricky part was reclaiming all the gold that they had once they left. But they had enough to survive for centuries.

"Dad, what's going to happen to us?" Logan asked.

"Nothing will happen to you. It's all up to God with what's going to happen to me," Dr. Rorja said.

"I don't want to lose you," Logan said.

"You'll never lose me, son. I'll always be there for you in one way or another," Dr. Rorja said.

Two hours later

"Alright, have all the arrangements been made?" Dr. Schrodhilt asked.

"Yes, the plane is being fueled and cleaned as we speak," Dr. Rorja said.

"Fantastic," Dr. Magnor said.

Just then the door was kicked open and a flash grenade was thrown in. Within seconds the entire room was enveloped in a thick smoke that had the room blinded. By the time the smoke cleared, they were all on the floor, handcuffed. The men then sat them in a chair.

"Which one of you is Dr. Rorja?" One of the men asked in a thick Tel Aviv accent.

Shit, the Israeli's got here first. This wasn't going to be good. Dr. Rorja thought as he nodded to them.

"We'll need to speak to you separately," the first man said.

"Why do you need to separate him?" Dr. Magnor asked.

"Because he is the reason you are in the position you're in right now. Without him, we would be chasing ghosts," the first man said.

"Dr. Rorja!" Dr. Schrodhilt said as things began to become more clear to him. "You, you're the reason the kids got away. I thought you said the kid made his decision," Dr. Schrodhilt continued.

"I did say that, but I never said what his decision was," Dr. Rorja said.

"He shot Dr. Spear. You were there specifically to make sure that didn't happen," Dr. Magnor said.

"He didn't shoot him, I did," Logan said as he stood up and addressed the council. "I'm sick and tired of hearing about everything you guys have and how it's never enough. You want to reduce the population of the world? Why? So you can have easier control over them? Isn't what you had enough?" Logan said.

"You know you are both dead men, right?" Dr. Magnor said.

"Shut up you," the first man said as he backhanded Dr. Magnor in the head.

"Do you have any idea who I am? That you lay your hands on me like that. I'll have your job, once my lawyers get a hold of you," Dr. Magnor said.

"Where you two are going, you're not going to need a lawyer. You're going to need a miracle," the first man said.

Just then the Americans and the British arrived in the room. When they saw the Israeli's there, they frowned. One man took his mask off.

"You were supposed to wait for us, assholes," the first American man said.

"Calm down. We were in the area," the first Israeli man said in jest. "You can take this man and his son into the other room to question him. We've got these two prepped for transport," the first man said as he smiled at the two men.

"Where are you taking us?" Dr. Schrodhilt asked.

"I wouldn't worry about that just yet," the first Israeli man said as he put a sack over Dr. Schrodhilt, Dr. Taros and Dr. Magnor's heads. Just then they started shaking violently and screaming.

"Give them something to calm down a bit," the American soldier said.

One of the SAS officers walked up to them and injected them with what Dr. Rorja could only imagine was Ativan. Instantly they both calmed down and slumped.

"What are you guys waiting for? Aren't you going to take me with them?" Dr. Rorja asked.

"We have something special for you," the SAS soldier said as he turned and smiled at Dr. Rorja. "We're going to have you disband this society, publically. While we've been here, the President of the United States has outed this organization as the top terrorist organization to man. Your role in helping Graham and his friends survive has granted you leniency with the international community. These men's assets, all of them will be frozen, pending further investigation and potentially redistributed. The best you can hope for is a witness protection program with enough money to live by, between you and your son. That's the best we can do," the man finished.

"I'll take it!" Dr. Rorja excitedly said. He was under the impression that he was going to be in a cell for the rest of his life, but a chance to start over, as a normal person with his son. A simple life. He couldn't imagine anything better than that.

"We'll get these two out of your way. Just so you know, we are combing each estate, each car, each plane, each bank vault, this entire building from top to bottom. Anything that is found in regards to this, or other human rights violations, will be used to the fullest extent in court. The death penalty is off the table. You all will have to live with the decisions you've made in life. May God have mercy on your soul," the first American Marine said.

Dr. Rorja was lead out of the room to his room where he and his son were granted time to pack for the upcoming International Tribune Court that had been called by the President. Dr. Rorja was as happy as he could be with the outcome of the raid and what they were offering him, but he couldn't help but wonder how it all went down with Graham after they lost all the evidence. How did they get the evidence? How did they get to the President? He was dying to know.

Chapter Twenty-Six

2 days prior

We pulled up in some bullshit town at a shady looking store to pick up some drug phones. Sorry, my anxiety is starting to get the best of me, and I don't have my microdoses here to relax. After this is all said and done, I'm going to therapy and going on some of that good shit. Lexapro, Zoloft. Sorry. I got out of the car and Jean handed me a wad of money, and I went inside and bought four cell phones as Larisa already had hers still on her wrist. I got back in the car and we got out of shady mcshadertown. The first thing I did is call up Conrad at Senna Ore.

"Graham, is that you? Where the hell have you been?" Conrad asked.

"Almost getting killed, you know, the usual," I said.

"He almost shot me in the head," Jean yelled into the phone from across the van.

"Shut up Jean," I said.

"Well anyway, I'm glad you're ok. Listen, we've had a breakthrough. Hannah is not completely OK, but she will be. You must come right away so we can discuss what happened," Conrad said.

"Change of plans, re-route to Senna in Newport," I said to Jackson.

"I'll just punch it into the GPS," Jackson started.

"No, don't do that. First, I don't think they'll come up, they're a bit off the radar; second, we don't want the GPS to have this when we return this hunky piece of shit back," I said.

"Roger that, so give me the address," Jackson said as I gave it to him.

"Conrad, can you tell me anything about what happened?" I asked.

"It's best you see for yourself. You're not going to be very happy, but it's the best we can do. It also worked for Franco. They've been in a safe room for the last few hours talking while being monitored. This seems to be working," Conrad said.

"Alright, well we're on our way. Be there in 2.5 hours," I said as I hung up the burner.

"What was that all about?" Larisa asked.

"Hannah is OK it seems. And Franco is awake," I said.

"Franco too? No shit," Jackson said.

"That's what they're telling me," I said.

"OK, so what's the next step," Rosette asked.

"I've been thinking about that neat little device on your wrist. Can it project?" I asked.

"It can if I add the attachment," Larisa said.

"Please," I said.

Larisa went into her purse and pulled out the attachment. She connected it to her wrist. She was now part cyborg. She projected her phone screen onto the door panel.

"What do you need?" She asked.

"Pull up the file we have on these people," I said.

Larisa opened her email and opened the attachment. We sat there for a little while reading through the documents. It was truly horrifying. It had everything, from the way that the idea first came about to have a global vaccine, to the depopulating the world's population and projections, to how money was funneled for research into this, to ways the news would push the vaccine since these people at the Consulate ran the mainstream media, to finally figuring out how they would use a jellyfish protein and mix it in the vaccine and inject it into people, to the two to three day latency period so nobody could track its genesis. I had to admit, in a sick and fucking twisted way, this was top level thinking here. The anti-vaccination crowd, which was growing by the day, would surely point to this in all future correspondence as to why you shouldn't be vaccinated. Before I read any of this, I couldn't dream this kind of stuff up.

"So, what do you want me to do with this?" Larisa asked.

"Can you draft an email on that thing?" I asked.

"Duh," She replied.

"OK, take dictation," I began.

To: WZ1826

From: Larisa@Protonmail.com

Subject: If you're still active, please answer

Hello. This is Graham Newsdon. You might recognize me as the one that took down the previous President. Well, this is the last email I had for the White House, so if someone is there, or if someone can get a message to President Rand Dotplum, please let me know. I know the answer to what's going on in the World. I won't get into it over the email, but I am going to meet with some people right now who are going to be able to explain to me exactly how to stop this 'sickness' that's been plaguing us. I know this is a longshot, but if someone is on the other end of the line, please get back to me. Thank you. —Graham.

Larisa read it back to me and I nodded. She sent it off.

"Great now, we wait," Jean said.

"Exactly," I said.

The rest of the car ride to Senna Ore was pretty quiet. We were all pretty gassed and could use a propofol night's rest. I zoned out, thinking about Hannah and how all I wanted in life was to have a wife and family. I'm sick of all the shit that I keep getting caught in. When we get through this, if we get through this, I'm going to take her on a Honeymoon, fuck it. A nice long two week honeymoon. I started thinking about the places that I would take her, and suddenly we pulled up to Senna. I nearly choked myself to death trying to unbuckle my belt as I slammed the side door open and rushed inside. Everyone slowly behind me.

"Where is she?" I asked as I rushed up to Dr. Pivarnick.

"She's safe, that's all you need to know at this exact moment. Graham, we have to talk about . . ." He said as I cut him off.

"I have to see her," I said.

"Ok but first . . ." Dr. Pivarnick tried again.

"No, I must see her," I said.

"Graham, listen to him please," Conrad said.

Something about the tone in his voice made me sit down in a chair and listen to his explanation. Conrad was right, this was going to shock the shit out of me.

"Firstly, you have to understand. That although she is better, she is not 'better.' She won't be for another three weeks," Dr. Pivarnick began.

"Why three weeks?" I asked.

"Just listen Graham. It's called Irukandji Syndrome. It comes from the sting of a jellyfish, a very particular kind of jellyfish. Mostly it's benign, sometimes there are side effects. Hypertension, abdominal pain, nausea, vomiting, sweating, pulmonary edema, on rare occasions, hypertension, cardiac arrest and possible heart failure. But this is not what was weaponized in these vaccines. In rare situations, there is an 'impending sense of doom' in the person. These people who are stung beg the doctor to end their life for them. This protein purified, caused people, all these people to take their own life. The sense that they weren't going to get better was so strong that the only thing they could do was end it. We have been able to locate it in the vial you brought us. Typically, these symptoms can take up to two weeks to clear up. Once we figured that out, we were able to replicate the vaccine with it in it and send one down to the CDC with instructions anonymously. We don't want them knowing we had anything to do with this. Next came the hard part, treating the victim," Dr. Pivarnick started.

"I don't understand, I thought you said it was over-powering. Why isn't Hannah being kept in a straightjacket or in a medically induced coma right now?" I asked.

"Listen Graham. At first we started small. We gave her 5 mg of Melatonin to see if we could get the Seroto-nin in her brain up and running. That didn't work at all, it only made her drowsy. Plus, you build a tolerance to Melatonin quickly. Next, we tried to step it up a little. We gave her a mix of Theanine, Hydroxytryptophan bet-ter known as 5-HTP, as well as St. Johns Wart and an Omega 3. That calmed her down for a few minutes, but then she started up again. So next we gave her a Keta-mine nasal spray stacked with an Oxytocin nasal spray. That seemed to work for twenty minutes, but then she was right back to where she was. Twenty minutes was unsustainable, plus again, the body builds tolerance to it," he paused for a moment.

"What happened next?" I asked.

"We put her in a medicated coma. We were hoping that after a few days she would fight off the protein. When we woke her, it was as if nothing happened and she was beside herself. We had to give her the spray treatments again just to calm her down enough to put her under again," he continued.

"But you said she would get better," I said.

"Irukandji Syndrome can last up to two weeks at the rough ends of it. Once we knew what we were dealing with, we knew we didn't have that kind of time. We were watching on the news that all sorts of people were killing themselves due to the 'sickness.' That's when an idea formed. Each microscopic destructive force leaves a signature. Whether it is side effects, or body changes, each will eventually give itself up. So, we started mapping out where the most people were being affected. What we found was very interesting. The global flu vaccine program was universal, but people seemed to be most affected in first World countries. Isn't that interesting? You would think that in third World countries they would be more affected, since they have worse living conditions, lower ironically enough vaccines. So why was this in the first world? United States, Great Britain, Israel, Spain, France, Dubai for example. Why?" He asked.

"I have no idea," I said.

"We started thinking about the role of fear in the human mind. What causes it, what prevents it? Certain rats when they smell Cat urine are scared off by the pheromones, which aids in saving their life. That's the fear in action that helps. But there are certain rats that become 'attracted' to cat urine, hovering around it. Their fear section in their brain is turned off. Granted it ends up with the cat eating them, but the lack of fear was what's interesting. These rats were infected with Toxoplasmosis," Dr. Pivarnick said.

He was right, I was not going to like that at all. "Wait a second, are you saying that you've given my wife Toxoplasmosis?" I asked incredulously.

"That's exactly what I'm saying Graham. The science behind it isn't quite understood yet, but if you look around the world, many first world countries don't have this problem. It's the third world countries that do. Nearly half of the entire world has Toxoplasmosis and they don't even know it. That's why the numbers weren't piling up in the third world countries," Dr. Pivarnick said.

"She can't just walk around with a parasite in her brain," I said.

"That parasite is what's keeping her alive, until her body can naturally fight off the protein that was injected in her," Dr. Pivarnick said.

"It's true Graham. This is our best chance to beat this thing. I mean just look at her," Conrad said.

I turned to look at Hannah, and she was laughing and smiling with Franco. I turned back to everyone else who were looking at me in disbelief.

"Are you telling me that I'm supposed to go to the leader of the free world, if he answers my email, but that's another story, and tell him that everybody needs to get infected with a parasite to keep them alive?" I asked.

"It sounds gross, but so many people have it that don't even know it. There have been studies done that people who have this tend to be risk takers, adrenaline junkies. It's not just a marker to spot AIDS in cat scans anymore. Also, yes, I think if we are to stop this on-slaught, we will need to do this. After two weeks, three weeks to be safe, the person would just take a prescription of Daraprim. Now that that piece of shit Martin Shkreli is in jail and no longer in charge of that company, the pricing for it is reasonable. This might even be called a World Crisis and you wouldn't have to pay for it," Dr. Pivarnick said.

I sat there and thought to myself for a little while what our options were. I couldn't deny that Hannah and Franco seemed to be the only two people that have survived the sickness. If I was going to go to the President with this information, I was going to need it to be solid. You don't just give a parasite to the entire world.

"Do you have all of this somewhere?" I asked.

"Absolutely. We charted everything down for you, everything that I've told you so far. We just can't have anything attached to us, you understand, right?" Conrad asked.

"I understand," I said.

Just then an email came through on Larisa's thingy. "Graham, listen to this," she said. "Hello Graham, I'm very glad to finally meet you in this sort of way, but that doesn't matter right now. We have a crisis between us, a very bad one, worse than anyone we've ever had maybe. If you have some information for me, I'd like you to come down to DC and see me. Bring your friends, I want them to brief my staff. What you have is too dangerous to send through the email. I look forward to seeing you tomorrow. You can reach me at this email at any time— Rand," she finished.

"Alright we know where we have to go. Can we bring her with us?" I asked.

"She's good to go, you just have to make sure she takes her medicine two weeks from today exactly as directed," Conrad said.

"Thank you," I said, as I turned and hugged both Dr. Pivarnick and Conrad. They had been so helpful over all this time with anything we've ever thrown at them.

I turned to everyone and smiled. Then I walked into the room where Hannah and Franco were, and when she saw me, she started to cry. She ran up to me and gave me a big hug and kiss. She asked me if I knew what was going on. Apparently, they kept her in the loop. I turned and talked to Franco for a minute and explained to him that his house burned down. He said it was fine, it wasn't his actual house anyway. It was a safe house as we predicted. He asked if we got what we came for, and I told him yes. We shook hands, and then I took Hannah's coat and put it around her. She grabbed her things from the corner, and I walked her out of the room. Once I did, everyone started clapping, Jean started whistling, that jackass. We all left together to get in the van. We had to get home and make sure we had everything together because we had to go to DC in the morning. Jean made a call and got the plane ready for an early AM take off. We got in the van, and I sat in the back with Hannah and wrapped my arms around her. It was amazing to me that this cat shit parasite was the only thing standing in the way between her and her offing herself.

Chapter Twenty-Seven

1 day prior

We didn't sleep that night. Our nerves were wrecked and the thought of what we had to do was just too important to not give it the attention we needed. At 6:00 a.m. we boarded the plane at Logan to DC. We wanted to go over what we were going to tell the President.

"Alright, so basically we're going to go in there and just show them the information we have. I'll do the talking," I said.

"Fair enough, he's familiar with you already. He might not want to talk to any of us anyway," Rosette said.

"How do you feel, baby?" I turned and asked Hannah.

"Aside from being tired, I actually feel kind of numb honestly," she replied.

"That's the parasite talking. Don't worry, we'll take good care of you," Jackson replied.

"Aw thanks Jax," Hannah said.

"There's going to be a car waiting for us at the airport," Larisa said.

"How do you know?" I asked.

"I just got an email from the President. I think he's expecting us a little later," Larisa said.

"Well email him back and tell him we'll be there around 9:30," I said.

"Roger that," she said and went to work on her hologram phone.

"So, we're all on the same page with what's going to go on?" I asked.

"Let's go over it one more time," Jean said as he sipped a morning mimosa.

"Alright, so we get in the car and go to the White House. They're probably going to bring us into a room with the joint chiefs of staff and sit us down. I'll show them Hannah first as the first 'cured' person. I'll explain it to them exactly like Dr. Pivarnick and Conrad explained it to us," I said.

"Sounds good. What could possibly go wrong?" Rosette asked.

We all just looked at her. Too much can go wrong. All the time, too much can go wrong as I've become very familiar with that feeling.

"Jean, I just wanted to say I'm sorry I pointed a gun at you," I said.

"I understand where you were coming from, mon ami. Maybe now, you understand the choice that I had to make to stay alive," he replied.

I had already come to terms with that feeling before, it was good to get that off my chest. But I think it finally clicked for Rosette.

"Jean, I'm sorry for what you went through and all the things I've been putting you through since you've been back. You saved our lives multiple times in Jerusalem, and the truth of the matter is without your generosity with your plane and your money, we wouldn't have gotten as far at all as we have so far. I truly forgive you," Rosette said.

A tear came to Jeans eye as he made his way over to Rosette and gave her a big hug. Finally, we were one big family again. This was the greatest gift I could ask for after almost losing my wife to this horrific bullshit.

Three hours later

We landed in DCA and got off the plane. There was an Escalade waiting for us. One-way bulletproof glass most likely. Windows tinted. Fully kitted out. This was a hot ride. But what did I expect? We were the belle of the ball right now in DC. Just nobody knew it yet.

"I'm special officer Mac. Welcome to DC. Please, get in the back," he said.

We obliged, and he got in the back with us. The entire car ride was very quiet. The special service agent was on point 100% of the time. I guess he didn't like surprises as much as we didn't either. After a while, we pulled up to the White House. There was police tape all around the front of the gate. We went around back to the secret underground entrance.

"What happened here?" I asked.

"Two people ran up to the white house with 9mm guns and pointed them at each other. They then started laughing hysterically, and then on cue, shot themselves in the head," Mac said.

"Was this the sickness?" I asked.

"Officially, we're still trying to determine that. It's so hard to pinpoint down exactly how to test for the sickness. But unofficially and off the record, yes it was," Mac said.

"So, the sickness has reached DC?" I asked.

"It has been in DC. Mostly in the hoity toity areas. We're still trying to figure that out," Mac said.

"Well that's why we're here. We're here to help explain all of that," I said.

"I recognized you from back in the day when you were at your brother's funeral on TV with the President. You know, when you first emailed him, he knew who you were, and he was terrified as to why you were reaching out to him. He'd been following the story closely, about how they set precedence with putting a sitting

President in jail, and how she had killed herself in jail. He almost didn't want to get involved," Mac said.

"She didn't kill herself?" I said.

"What do you mean?" Mac asked.

"I was there the day before. Without her help, I wouldn't have been able to figure a few things out regarding all of this. They silenced her," I said without hesitation.

"Jesus Christ," Mac said.

We went through the underground tunnel and parked. We got out and a few other secret service agents met us. They were talking into their earpieces, and I overhead one of them say the package has been delivered. I only thought people talked that way in movies. Fuck me if I'm wrong.

"Please follow us," Mac said.

We made our way through the tunnels and finally came up into the White House. They led us through a corridor, then another corridor, then finally into the main room.

"Please wait here for a minute," Mac said as he turned and talked to the other secret agents. They nodded and then dispersed. Mac turned back to us and motioned with his head to follow him. We walked down another corridor and turned the corner and walked into the meeting room. There were all the bigshots. Top military generals, the President and some cabinet members.

"Welcome Graham and welcome to your friends. I'm happy you're here. How are you liking it so far?" President Dotplum asked.

"Everytime I come to this city, it's for tragic reasons, so I'm not really sure," I replied.

Everybody looked at me like I had three heads on my body.

"Understandable," the President said.

"I see that the sickness has hit outside the White House," I replied.

"Yeah, what happened outside. Terrible tragedy. Possibly the biggest tragedy that's ever happened in front of the White House," President Dotplum said. "But enough about that. Which one of you is Larisa?" He asked.

"I am," she said.

"You know that you've been on our radar for a while now. Your computer skills are extraordinary. You're one of a kind," the President said.

Larisa blushed. "Thank you, Mr. President," she said.

"Enough with the introductions. As you can see, we have a big crisis, possibly the biggest crisis that we've ever faced as a planet. I was told that you have some information for me?" The President said and turned to me.

"Well Mr. President," I began. I then went into great details about how the Rorja's contacted me after my wedding and sent us on this wild chase. I explained to him everything that we had been up to, up to this moment. I told him about the Consulate, and Dr. Spear. I told him about how Dr. Rorja saved our lives, despite him more than likely being killed or jailed in the future. I also introduced him to Hannah and explained to them what happened to her at Bionic.

"Hold on a minute, so you're telling me that you've caught this thing and survived it?" The President asked.

Hannah nodded.

I then continued and explained to him how Hannah had indeed caught it, but that there was a company that we worked with, that happened to be Jean's second cousin that we gave a vial of the vaccine to. They were able to reverse engineer it and locate a protein in it from the Irukandji Jellyfish. I explained to him the side effect of the jellyfish sting, and how it had been weaponized to create a suicidal population. Then I went into detail about everything that Dr. Pivarnick did to try to heal Hannah, and what they finally came up with. The President was less than pleased with what I said.

"Hold on a minute. Are you telling me that you injected a parasite into her and that's the only thing keeping her from killing herself?" The President asked.

"I'm saying that exactly. Irukandji syndrome usually lasts up to two weeks, but we're keeping her infected for three. Then we will cure it, and everything will be fine," I said.

The President ruffled his combover. "So, you're suggesting that we infect the entire population with Toxoplasmosis in order to stop them from killing themselves?" He turned and asked.

I turned to the head Doctor in the room. "This has already been sent to the CDC for analysis and containment. Is anything that I've said so far sensible?" I asked.

The head Doctor turned to the President. "Mr. President, everything that's been said here so far is entirely plausible. It's an ingenious idea really. There are few outer symptoms if any of Toxoplasmosis. The truth is that half the World's population has it. In fact, it seems to be a third world problem. That could be why only the first World countries have been affected for the most part," the head Doctor said.

"How exactly would we deploy something like this? This was a global vaccine," the President said.

"If I may, Mr. President, for a minute." The entire room turned around as a familiar voice came through. It was Vice President Wade Granny. The press had fallen in love with him as he was the major reason that the legalization of Marijuana went through earlier that year. Finally, what began with William Randolph Hearst demonizing and coining the term of Cannibus as Marijuana in his papers more than a century ago, had finally come full circle. People in his inner circles called him AHL. No, not the Hockey League, but for 'A Hemp License.' Many just called him Hemp lovingly.

"Well good to see you Hemp, what brings you here?" The President asked.

"I thought you two were never supposed to be in the same room together for national security purposes," Rosette said.

Everybody turned to look at her as if she had unleashed a load of diarrhea into her pants.

"That's OK young lady. Everybody still thinks I'm at Camp David. I was brought here covertly. I needed to be here to hear all about this. Once I found out that we almost had a cure, I couldn't stop myself. I hope I'm not intruding," Wade said.

"Not at all Hemp. These kids just told us everything they know. The General will bring you to speed while we figure things out," the President said.

"So, what do you think?" I asked the President.

"Right, so that's where we were. I want to hear from Neurology first. Can someone bring her in please?" The President asked.

This slender middle-aged woman with thick round glasses came in. She introduced herself as Dr. Hochman. She was head of Neurology and Neuropharmacology at George Washington University. She told us that she had been trying to figure out how to test the brains of those who had been lost to the sickness, but nothing was coming up.

"Dr. Hochman. Can you advise how long you've been working this up?" The President asked.

"About three weeks now," Dr. Hochman said.

"Uh huh, and are you any closer to figuring any of this out?" The President asked.

"Unfortunately, no. Toxicology takes weeks to come back and neural CT's and MRI's came up normal so far. My hands are tied," she said.

"I see. Dr. Hochman what if I were to tell you that you were in the presence of a young woman who has been cured of this apocalyptic issue?" The President asked.

Her eyes got as wide as hockey pucks. "How is that possible?" She asked.

Hannah stood up and introduced herself. She turned to Hemp and asked him to listen because she was going to go through everything. Very slowly, my loving wife commanded the most intense room on the entire planet Earth with ease, as she went through the story about getting 'infected' at Bionic. She walked them all painstakingly through how they went to a secret facility, where she was tied down to a gurney and had her head covered in wires monitoring her brain waves. She then went into the part that I could barely stomach. The part where out of nowhere, the 'sickness' took over and she just had a complete loss for life. She tried to break free of the gurney and grab anything that could make her pain go away. Pills, a scalpel, a needle, anything. She said that the pain was so strong that she couldn't believe a God that created us could have created a sensation like that. She then told them that she went to bed, and when she woke up, she was in a straitjacket. She begged the Doctors to end her life for her. She said describing the horror and pain of this was kind of like explaining a hallucinogenic trip. Sometimes there's no words created that can be used to describe it. She then went into a controlled coma for a short time at which point the Doctors came up with a plan. That's when she, in detail explained to the neurologist the steps that I heard Dr. Pivarnick took with her. From the Theanine, all the way up to Toxoplasmosis. She said that once she was infected with this parasite, within thirty minutes it wasn't like she was better or happy, but she was completely dull. Unafraid of anything, numb. Like how they keep maniacs sedated through medication. She made it abundantly clear to Dr. Hoffman that the Ketamine and Oxytocin worked for a brief time, but then once the veil was lifted again, she was twice as bad.

Everybody sat there and hung onto her every word. All eyes were focused on Hannah. Once she was done, she sat back down, and all eyes focused on Dr. Hochman.

"Dr. Hochman, does this story hold up?" The President asked.

"I have to say, it never occurred to me to use a live sample to alter anything. I am familiar with all the rat and mice trials that show when infected with Toxoplasmosis Gondii, they become extremely unafraid of anything. What's the prognosis for you Hannah?" The Doctor asked.

"I was told that this syndrome, this Irukandji syndrome can last for up to two weeks, maybe longer because it was genetically modified. I was told that I had to carry this in my brain for two weeks, then go on medicine for a few weeks, then get an MRI and CT to confirm it's been cleared out," Hannah said.

"Dr. Hochman, what exactly is the treatment for this?" The President asked.

"Typically Primethamine and Sulfadiazine. Wait, are you seriously considering infecting this entire planet with Toxoplasmosis?" The Doctor asked wildly as if it finally clicked in her head.

"We are losing hundreds of thousands of people every couple of days. In front of us is the only living person who has ever come back from the brink so to speak. We need to keep all options on the table," Hemp interjected.

"I don't think there's enough Daraprim and Sulfadiazine for every single person," the Doctor said.

"Maybe not right now, but we'll have about a month to generate enough," the President said.

"If that's what you think is best, I'll alert the WHO and the CDC," the Doctor said.

"We'll do that Dr. Hochman, thank you. That is all," the President said.

Dr. Hochman turned to leave, and the President called out to her. "Dr. Hochman."

"Yes?"

"I hope you understand that this is national security. We cannot let this cat out of the bag. You cannot speak to anybody about this," the President sternly warned.

"Yes, Mr. President," she said as she turned and left, secret service following behind.

The President rubbed his head and put his hands on the table, in typical power move fashion.

"I want to know who did this. I was told you have some information for me?" He asked.

"Can I project onto that projector?" Larisa asked.

"Please," the President replied.

"Here, why don't you sit down over here, it's easier," Hemp said.

"Thank you," Larisa said.

She fiddled with her projector on her wrist and put it up on the screen. The General turned the lights off. She opened the email that she was going to send to the President, when she was asked not to. She opened the file.

We let the documents that we uncovered speak for themselves. Very slowly they began reading all the secret documents. I never actually saw this until now. It talks about some ancient secret societies and some information about 'signs from the sky.' It went into detail about Saturn losing its rings, and the artificial Sun being created, which sparked this. It goes back to the ancient Sun and Planet worship, that I was very familiar with. The parties in the room seemed to ignore that part. Larisa swiped and flipped the page. It went into very dire details about how a plague needed to be unleashed onto man. That Christians would be convinced it was the rapture. That Jews would be convinced the Messiah was coming back. That Islam would be convinced that it was the great war. Once the population was depleted well enough, they would institute the cure, as long as people signed away their rights to a one world government. Once that was done, a new religion would be slowly brought into consciousness, one for everybody. This would be the Age of Aquarius. They weren't worried about it taking hold, religions seldom take hold right away, and initially it's a very violent revolution once a religion begins to be introduced. These elites, they had all the time and money in the world. They were just continuing something that their ancestors had done. Larisa flipped the page again. This time they named themselves, the heads of the Consulate. The Schrodhilts, the Magnors, the Dotpuns, the Rorjas, the Taros, and the Spears countless other 'super families' that were on board with this. They spoke about their search for the perfect way to take the lives. It couldn't be a violent outside force, people would band against it. It couldn't be a poisoning, that could be backtracked. The key was for people to take their own lives in mass quantities. Nobody would be able to pin that on anybody. One of them suggested a global vaccine initiative. The flu was the most obvious target. Countless people had already talked to the Presidents of each country about adopting this. The only thing left was how were they going to be able to delay the flu vaccine long enough so that it couldn't be traced back to it. Also, how were they going to be able to put something in the vaccine that would cause mass suicide. Larisa flipped the page. It just so happened that Dr. Spear went on a vacation with one of his mistresses to Japan. There he witnessed someone getting bit by a jellyfish and come to shore. After a little while, the man started acting very irrational and started smashing a rock over his head. Curious, Dr. Spear wandered over to the man and asked him what happened? The man asked him to kill him and put him out of his misery. Dr. Spear then collected the jellyfish and brought it back with him to a Lab in Geneva, where he knew some scientists on some black box programs and asked them to extract its 'venom.' It didn't have venom, but they were able to isolate the jellyfish. It's called Irukandji Syndrome and it comes from a specific type of box jellyfish. Larisa flipped the page. Scientists worked on isolating this protein in its sting that causes this syndrome. At first, they were able to have their projected outcome happen every two weeks. Then after genetically modifying the protein, they were able to have it have the requested effect every ten days. Another three weeks went by and they finally were able to have a person respond every two days. Dr. Spear was pleased. He then brought his findings to the consulate, and they deliberated on how to make this go viral, no pun intended. They came up with the universal flu vaccine that had been championed by so many. Larisa turned to the final page. This described the projected outcomes of it being latent in the human body versus when it would affect. It also projected the amount of people lost. The one big difference from their projection and what actually happened, was that those in third world countries and the poorest cities and states were significantly less affected than those that were in the first World areas.

"And that's when our scientists figured out the vaccine's weakness. It only hit the wealthy areas, so that's when they decided to try with toxoplasmosis," I said to the President.

The President rolled his eyes and looked at his cabinet. "What do you think Hemp?" He asked his VP.

"I think we have a small window of time to act, and we should definitely work on this. I'd like to see this tested in real time though," the VP said.

"Alright, we'll get a live subject. Can you get Neurology back in here?" The President asked.

The secret service left the room in search of Dr. Hochman.

"Well Graham, ladies and gents. If this works, you will be instrumental in avoiding the largest 'plague' since the Spanish Flu. Of course, we cannot have anyone know who you are for National Security purposes," the President said.

"Of course," I said. It was funny to me. The last time I was in the White House I was shit drunk and having the President of the United States grill me about my brother's mission in Syria. Now I was no longer the enemy of the Presidency, but its greatest ally.

Ah good, Dr. Hochman, you're back. Let me cut the bullshit and get straight to it. We're going to get you a live sample, and we want you to infect them with Toxo," the President said.

"What if . . ." Dr. Hochman began.

"What if what?" The President asked.

"What if this isn't the key?" Dr. Hochman asked.

"We'll deal with that when it comes up."

We talked and waited for an hour or two until we got word that there was a patient in the lab in the basement. We all got up, and the secret service followed us as we made our way into the basement of the White House. If you've never been in the basement before, let me tell you it's like a functioning city down there.

"Who is this?" The President asked.

"We caught him downtown D.C. banging his head into a storefront window. When the police picked him up, he was begging them to kill him."

"Jesus Christ. This is terrifying," Dr. Hochman said.

"We need your help in saving the world Doctor," the VP said.

The Doctor scrubbed up and went into the room where this man was being kept. He was in a straight-jacket and strapped down to the gurney. The next moments were a bit of a blur on account of the adrenaline that was being passed around the room like a hot potato. However, she eventually injected him with Toxo, and we waited.

"What's the latency period for this?" The VP turned and asked me.

"It's two days for the 'sickness' to take form. It can take 10-23 days after eating exposed meat, and about five days after handling cat feces," I said.

"You a doctor or something?" The President asked.

"Almost was," I said as once again I reflected on my life since everything took form when my brother died.

"We don't have that kind of time!" The VP said.

"Relax, we're injecting this patient directly with it. It won't even be half that time," I said.

We watched as Dr. Hochman injected this patient with the Toxo. She stepped back and took her gloves off and her mask, and sat on a chair in the corner. Now we wait.

Not an hour went by, and the patient stopped crying and screaming. He started to sweat a little and complained about muscle aches. Which was a good sign, because that's the symptoms that one would get when infected with Toxo. Another half an hour went by and finally the patient spoke up.

"Doctor, could I have a glass of water?" He asked.

Dr. Hochman looked over to us and cocked her head. The President nodded. She went to the corner of the room and grabbed a paper cup and filled it with water for this man.

"Could you help me out of this please?" The man asked.

Once again, she looked at the President for advisement. He turned to his secret service and nodded as they entered the room to make sure this man wouldn't go apeshit. Dr. Hochman undid the straps and took off the straitjacket. The man very calmly took the cup of water and pounded the whole thing down and set it aside.

"I feel achy," the patient said again as he lay down on the gurney and closed his eyes and appeared to be trying to fall asleep.

"Graham, you and your people might have done it. You son of a bitch!" President Dotplum said as he turned to me. Everybody started high fiving and getting excited.

"This needs to get out to everybody immediately," the VP said.

The room started discussing plans on getting this information throughout the World.

"But what about the people who caused this. If you alert the WHO, NATO, etc., you will just drive them underground," I said.

Everybody just froze and looked over at me. They didn't consider that. This entire ordeal has been such a horrifying thing for everybody, that the moment got ahead of us.

"Graham is right. We need to discuss this first," the President said.

"We should use our guys, MI6 and the Israeli's, the VP said.

"You said at one point that this Dr. Rorja saved your life?" The President asked me.

"His two sons tried to prevent all of this but were killed by these people. Dr. Rorja and his only remaining son were with us on the beach in Boston when he saved our lives. We wouldn't be here without him," I said.

"Larisa, I need you to locate his email and send him an email telling him that we're coming and to keep everyone there," the President said.

"On it," she replied.

"Graham. Your help has been incredible. Nobody has been more helpful than you. But we need to take this to the War Room. Secret Service will drop you guys off at your hotel," the President said as he turned and shook my hand.

"Thank you, Mr. President," I said.

I turned to my friends who were too awestruck to speak this entire time we've been here. "Guys, let's go have a good night," I said.

"You got it Graham," Jackson said.

"Tres bien, mon ami," Jean said.

"I could use a drink," Hannah said.

We all laughed.

The Secret Service took us back to the Hilton in Downtown DC. We were just going to have to wait until the President made his speech tomorrow.

Never apologize for being correct, or for being ahead of your time. If you're right and you know it, speak your mind. Even if you are a minority of one, the truth is still the truth —Mahatma Gandhi

Chapter Twenty-Eight

We woke up after a night of heavy drinking. Well, I didn't, but they sure had fun. Everyone was hungover. I ran down the hallway to refill the ice bucket and picked up a gallon of orange juice from the cubby of shit to eat and drink that hotels have. I made my way to pick up a few cups and was on my way. I got back in the hotel room.

"Oh, God, Newdson, you are my savior," Rosette said as she poured a cup of OJ and took it to the face. Everyone shortly followed suit.

"It's almost time for the President's speech. Should we turn on Blur?" I asked.

"Do we have to?" Hannah asked.

"Yes, we do," I said as I turned Blur on.

"I just want to say to my fellow patriots and loving Christians across the Country, I have very high level intel that we're about to get some great news. Now, I

can't come out and say it yet, but as we wait for the President to take the stand, I want to remind all of you that evil cannot win in the end. It's not how this works. Here comes the President, I'll shut up now," Blur said.

My fellow American's and freedom lovers around the World. We have been under the spell and guise of a monolithic ruling force that has managed to take our will to live away from us. For national security purposes I cannot share when we learned, or how we learned, but just know that this country owes you all a great debt of gratitude. This is a matter of National Security. Possibly the biggest matter of National Security that there ever was. A little while back you all remember that people started committing suicide and we were unable to stop them. By the time one person got into this frenzied state of mind, it was too late. That was the case until last night, when unfortunately for National Security purposes I can't tell you who, but last night I was introduced to a young lady who had this 'disease', so to speak, and was cured of it. Myself and my cabinet met this lovely lady, very beautiful, very lovely, at the White House. She had explained to us how a small group of scientists had cured her. Naturally I was very skeptical, the top minds in this Country were nowhere near able to make the same claim. Until we captured a live test subject and did exactly what they said to do. I saw this man, cured of it in front of my eyes. That's why I, along with my staff and the Vice President, have come up with emergency centers where you can be treated for this. For national security purposes, we cannot disclose the viral agent that was found in the global flu vaccine, but we can assure you that it will not be a problem for you anymore. Within the next 24 hours, this cure will be available to all the CVS's, Walgreens et cetera. Some side effects will be a slight fever and some muscle aching, but believe me when I tell you, it's better than the alternative. After two weeks there will be a set of medications that you need to take in order to flush the reactant out of your system. After that, everybody should be fine, and we can go about our merry lives. Earlier this morning I spoke with our lovely allies in Great Britain as well as Israel, which were hit as well. We have sent joint task forces out to remove these people who committed these heinous crimes. Due to the nature of their crimes, an International Tribune has been created to try them in a secret court and banish them so that we will never hear from them again. Their assets are also being seized as we speak by the British and Swiss governments as well as all their offshore accounts. We

will never have to worry about these people again. Unfortunately, that is all the information I have for right now. Thank you to all you tireless Hospital workers, and lab techs, who have been working overtime to stop this plague of national and international crisis. God bless you, and God bless America.

"Well there you have it folks, straight from the horse's mouth, so to speak. We'll be providing coverage of this all day, so don't go anywhere," Blur said.

We watched the President disappear into the White House and not two minutes later my phone rang. I didn't recognize the number.

"Hello?" I said.

"Put me on speakerphone Graham," the President said.

I did as instructed.

"There's a reason that at the CIA there are no names on the walls of the lost, only stars. What you have done for your country yesterday, for this planet, for the good of humanity, it may have been the greatest thing anybody has ever done. Believe me, I know," the President began.

"Thank you, Mr. President," I said.

"Jean," the President began.

"Oui?" He replied.

"Consider your record clean. I had a chance to review it. This Country owes you a debt of gratitude. And be sure to let your cousin know that all his work, although he will never get credit for it, will never be forgotten," the President said.

"How did you know?" Jean asked bewildered.

"Are you familiar with Smartdust technology?" The President joked.

All at once I knew what happened. When Larisa sprayed Jackson and me at Bionic Edge, we were covered with GPS trackers. Once we reached out to Lilac's old email address, they must have geo-located us. Based on the information I said to him, he must have known.

"I do have to tell you Graham, I've heard your life story so many times I feel like it's my own. We are well aware of everything that you're into, what you've gotten into. You're one of the great unsung heroes of the 21st century. But perhaps I can give you on behalf of your Country a little gratitude," the President said.

"How's that?" I asked.

"We're going to pay for your honeymoon. Anywhere you want to go, all included," the President said.

"Holy shit! That's amazing Mr. President. Thank you so much."

"Please, call me Rand," he said.

"Thank you, Rand," I said.

"And thank you to your whole team. I was never much of a science guy growing up, but what I saw yesterday was truly as close to a miracle as I've ever seen," he said as he hung up.

I hung up the phone and looked and smiled at Hannah. She was still having some stiffness. Her fever seemed to be fading.

"You know, they're going to write a story out of this one day," Rosette said.

"I hope they make me jacked and beautiful," Jackson said.

"You are jacked you donkey. Let's go home," I said.

"Agreed," Jean said as he turned and made a call. We were going to head for Reagan to get the fuck out of dodge.

Don't just teach your children to read, teach them to question what they read. Teach them to question every-thing. —George Carlin

Chapter Twenty-Nine

2 weeks later

I kept in touch with the President for a few weeks just to make sure he didn't need anything from me and to find out what happened. It turned out that these men are cur-rently holed up so far below ground that they'd be able to survive a nuclear bomb. When I asked about Dr. Rorja, the President told me that in exchange for his co-operation, they were going to put him and his son in the witness protection program. Good for him, I thought. A fresh start. Live a life like a real person. Sure, the deci-sions he had made previously he was one day going to have to answer to his maker for. But he did save our lives, and I won't soon forget that. They never explained what the new injection was, it would cause widespread panic. Sometimes what the public doesn't know is best, I thought. The smart ones would figure out by the medi-cine they had to take, and maybe a handful of people would be able to reverse engineer the symptoms to the drug, do some research and figure it out. Of course, they would never have proof, but that's beside the point. It reminded me of what Dr. Cortese told me that those beings in the sky said to me. "The discovery of Alien Life would come as a shock to the population. Humans would finally realize that we are not alone. Moreover, many people would start abolishing their religions as some religions preach that their God has created only Humans and would not create any other life forms. If in any case they turn out to be more advanced than us, then Global Unity would finally be achieved. However, a significant population needs to want for it. As long as religion rules the planet and people who fight for exposing higher beings are killed off, there will be no contact. It was a little disappointing, but I understood why. But here's the best part.

"What are you writing, baby?" Hannah asked.

"Just some notes for my new book," I said.

"You haven't made a video in a while," she replied.

"Yeah, I figure I'd let this global pandemic thing settle down for a little while then do what I can," I said.

"Are you ready?" She asked.

"Hell, yeah I'm ready," I said.

It's honeymoon time bitches!

Chapter Thirty

1 week later

We decided to take our honeymoon to LA and San Diego. I know right? Out of all the places I've been to, that we've been to, flown to, I've never been to LA. I've always wanted to go there. Truth was, when I was younger, I used to be an actor. From like 14-17. Was in a few commercials here and there. Helped pay for some of my school. Anyway, we landed in LA a little while ago. Hannah was so excited. It had been two weeks since she was infected with the parasite, and she just finished taking her medication for it. She was clear and free. Best feeling in the World.

We started by having lunch, and then made our way to Hollywood Boulevard to see the stars. We are all made of star material, which is why we call children young-sters or youngSTARS. That's where it comes from. We found our favorite actors and took pictures.

Then we went to the Comedy Store. Sam Tripoli was on. Full time comedian, full time karate master. I looked around the club and it was full of gorgeous women, some were holding signs. I'd never seen something like that before. Then we made our way across town to Kevin Smith's 'Hollywood Babble On' live taping of his podcast. He actually read my comment, the audience got a laugh out of it. We then went out for dinner and then went to bed.

Day 2

We walked around taking pictures of the Hollywood sign and stopped in Beverly Hills. One of my brother's favorite shows was Beverly Hills 90210. I was a little young for it, but he would have been thrilled to know I was there. We had lunch at a little boutique, and Hannah went clothes shopping. Hell, if this was going to be on the government's tab, we were going to make it count. We then went to Mulholland Drive and took pictures of everything. After that, we went to Disney. I know, a lot to do in one day.

Day 3

We spent this entire day at Disney. We didn't get half of what we wanted to get done the night before, so we went back. Seeing Hannah smile as she took pictures with Mickey and the cast lit up my life. We grabbed a quick lunch, at which point there was a television. We hadn't seen one in a while. The NEWS was talking about how the amount of suicides had drastically fallen in all the problematic areas. What worried me was the amount of people that were infected with the sickness but

weren't getting treated. It's scary to think how many people on this planet live with this parasite in their brain,
without knowing a thing. Feeling like their personality is
theirs, until they get treated and find out they are less ad-
venturous and more conservative. Must come as a shock
to many people. Satisfied with our lunch, we left and did
a tour of a movie set, that the President had set up for us.
We had the entire lot to ourselves. This is what living
like a star truly is, I thought to myself as we watched an
episode of 'The Good Doctor' being filmed. We made
our way back to the hotel, when something stuck in the
back of my mind. There was something that Dr. Spear
had said that had really bothered me. About me not
knowing what was happening in parts of the World. I
tried to shrug it off, but as I sipped on my hot tea in the
hotel room, the thought invaded my brain like that parasite. I tried to shrug it off as I went to sleep.

Day 4

We decided to rent a car and drive down to San Diego. I'd never been to the beaches there, or the Aquarium
and Zoo. That last part was all Hannah. She loves animals. We got in the car and made the few hour drive
down to San Diego and set up shop at the Hilton. We got
in our bathing suits and lay out by the pool for a little
while. Then we walked a few blocks down to the beach

and set up shop. Hannah had snuck some Margaritas with her in some water bottles. It was only us. Fuck it. I had one with her and we smiled as we worked on our tans.

After falling asleep for a few hours, we went back to the hotel and showered and got ready to go to the Aquarium. When I tell you this Aquarium was gorgeous, that's exactly what I mean. I've never seen Hannah so happy. After satisfying her animal cravings there, we went to the Zoo. We walked around until we saw a cage with two bears. They were snuggling in a long metal tube. The male woke up, got up and walked into the middle of the field and took a ginormous steamy shit. It smelled the entire place up. We just laughed. After we were done there, we made our way back to the hotel room where we lay down and talked, until we fell asleep.

Day 5

I was awoken by a call from Larisa. She had told me that Dr. Cortese was trying to reach me and that he could be reached at a very specific number. I hung up with her and gave him a call.

"Hello?" I said.

"Hello Graham. I'm told you're on your honeymoon? How is that going?" He asked.

"It's going great actually. Listen, is everything OK?" I asked.

He was silent for a moment. "Do you remember that message that I read you over the phone over the holidays about what they said?" He asked.

"I do. Is everything ok?" I asked.

"We just received an identical message to the first. But it seems that the first was incomplete. It seems that there were people with vested interest in scrambling that message. Would you like to know what the rest of the message said?" He asked.

I rolled over and woke Hannah up. She seemed like she was enjoying a dream and was a little cranky that I had woken her. Oh well. I put the phone on speaker.

"You're here with me and Hannah," I said.

"Graham, they mentioned that there would be no contact until said problems went away. But what they didn't get a chance to tell you was that there were some that were already here. Hiding in a DUMB, and they're not exactly the friendliest group," Dr. Cortese said.

"What's a DUMB?" Hannah asked.

"Deep underground military base," I said turning to her. "But wait, Dr. Cortese. Where are they located. How is this even possible?" I asked.

"They have been here for hundreds of years. They have the ability to feed off of energy, mostly fear and anger. They won't tell us where it is, but they said if you look to maps that 'show what should have been impossible for the time,' you will see it. They say that this is what is literally holding our civilization back," Dr. Cortese said.

"Do you need us to come to San Jose?" I asked.

"That won't be necessary. But from what they've said, they've told us that another attack is imminent, and we need to locate this base. They said that it would be buried next to the greatest discovery mankind would have ever found, and a wealth of knowledge that would be innumerable. It would activate some de-activated DNA strands in our body if we got a hold of it," Dr. Cortese said.

"Do we know what it is?" I asked.

"The Library of Alexandria was not destroyed. It was moved," Dr. Cortese said.

Coming June 15, 2021

Into the Rabbit Hole
The Hidden Archives
By Micah T. Dank

The Hidden Archives, Book Five, the continuation of *Into the Rabbit Hole*: Fresh off their last adventure that nearly took Graham's newly wedded wife from him, they are thrown once again into a mystery as old as most religions. The Library of Alexandria has not been burned down but moved to a secret location. A hacked computer ropes Graham into this new adventure and once he located the Library, he can finally finish his book series proving that the Bible is nothing more than a veiled Astrology book. If he survives his own demons.

For more information
visit: www.SpeakingVolumes.us

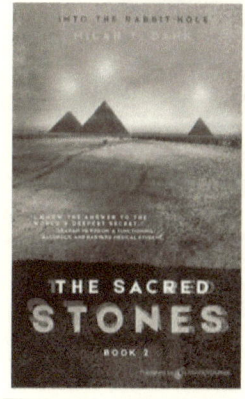

On Sale Now!

"Irving's writing is relaxed and authentic and takes readers inside a compelling world of legal and social issues…"—Bruce Kluger, columnist, *USA Today*

For more information
visit: www.SpeakingVolumes.us